ACCIDENTAL DAD

LOVE IN LITTLE LOBO
BOOK 2

Elaine Grant

I0536819

Table of Contents

COPYRIGHT

Accidental Dad
LOVE IN LITTLE LOBO
BOOK 2
This is a work of fiction.
Names, characters, places and incidents are either the product of the author's imagination or are used fictitiously, and any resemblance to actual persons, living or dead, business establishments, events or locales is entirely coincidental.

• • • •

Art Image Rights:
AleksandarNaki Istock.com 641332810 Family
Brenda Bailey Shutterstock.com 1495496 Victorian house
Antony84 Istock.com Stock photo ID:489387274 Grey dog running away
Welcomia Shutterstock.com 109596224 Montana's Rocky Mountains.
Published 2019 by Mountain Writer Publishing
[Originally published 2008 as *An Ideal Father*]

CHAPTER ONE

June

"NOW YOU JUST STAY there for a minute. Everything will be all right."

The low, gruff voice came from outside the construction trailer where Cimarron Cole was working at a paper-strewn desk. Frosty air from a window air conditioner blasted the side of his face and ruffled his hair, but at least it beat the stifling humidity outside. Cimarron glanced at the large clock on the opposite wall as the doorknob turned.

Cimarron's brother, R.J., popped his head around the door, a sheepish look on his face. "Hey, little bro. Late again. Sorry."

"Yeah, I've heard that before. Get to work. You've put the painters behind schedule already."

"Well, see, ah..." R.J. screwed up his mouth and glanced behind him. "I've got a little problem."

Cimarron waited in silence. R.J. had a lot of little problems. He was good-looking, with curly dark hair and the Cole family's legendary doe-brown eyes that women couldn't seem to resist. The thirty-eight-year-old still considered himself a ladies' man. Well, at least until the past few years, when he'd been forced to slow down.

"You see, Erica ran out on me this morning. Left me. Told me to...Well, you probably can figure out what she told me."

Cimarron grunted and made an impatient gesture with his hand. "So, what's new? You trade girlfriends like most people trade cars. And come inside—you're wasting energy and letting the cool air out, to boot."

R.J. twisted around in the doorway and motioned. A five-year-old miniature R.J. stepped hesitantly into the tiny office. R.J.'s son, Wyatt.

1

Cimarron tensed. What now? Why the hell had he caved and hired his brother on this project?

"See, she just up and left. And I ain't got nobody to watch Wyatt, so I thought maybe he could sit here while you..."

Cimarron's jaw clenched and he shoved his chair back and went around the desk, taking R.J. by the arm and forcing him outside onto the narrow stoop. Cimarron shut the door and they faced off with their chests almost touching.

"You think I'm going to *babysit* for you today? No way in hell. I have got work coming out my ears. I'll be here till midnight as it is. I told you when you talked me into taking you on, you had to be reliable."

R.J. pressed back against the porch rail to put another inch between himself and his brother. "Okay, okay. But I'm here now, just a few minutes—"

"Over an hour late! And dragging your kid with you."

"Look, I'll have a sitter by tomorrow. Hell, Erica might be back by then. He ain't going to bother you. I swear, he'll sit right there in that chair."

"No. You just go home for the day. I'll get somebody to finish painting the molding."

"That's not right, Cimarron. I need the money. More than ever now, if I gotta hire a sitter. Just let him stay in there while you work. I'll hurry and look for a sitter over my lunch hour."

Cimarron's shoulders sank at R.J.'s imploring look. Nothing but problems. The whole family. All his life. Nothing but problems.

R.J. grinned. "You've always been a good little brother."

"Yeah, I've always been a pushover," Cimarron said. "You get your work done this morning and come get him. You know I don't know a damn thing about kids."

"He's a good boy. Won't give you a lick of trouble. And you gotta admit he's pretty cute," R.J. said, winking, with a lilt of pride in his voice.

"He looks a hell of a lot like you."

R.J. grinned. "And that means he looks just like you, too."

That much was true. Cimarron and R.J. could have passed for twins, except for the four-year difference in their ages.

"I'll be back for him in a couple of hours."

R.J. bounded off the porch and trotted along the tree-lined allée leading to Cimarron's current restoration project, a grand antebellum plantation house. Once finished, the home would be the crowning glory, so far, in his body of work.

A sultry Louisiana breeze drifted by, stirring the leaves of an overhanging oak branch, leaving Cimarron's skin hot and sticky. He longed to suck in the cool, clean air of Idaho, but he'd been gone so long now the place didn't seem like home anymore. Besides, there was nothing left there for him. No home, no family. Even R.J. didn't know where their good-for-nothing father was—or so he said. And the sad thing was, Cimarron doubted his brother would be around for Wyatt any more than their own father had been around for them, once the rodeo bug bit him again and he got bored with "daddying."

The phone ringing in the trailer caught his attention and he ducked back inside. Wyatt perched on the chair in the corner, watching Cimarron's every move with wary eyes.

"Hello," Cimarron said into the receiver, his gaze wandering to avoid looking at the child as he listened to the voice on the other end of the phone.

"Cimarron Cole?"

"Yes, who's this?"

"Bobby James. We met at the casino in New Orleans last year."

Cimarron frowned, trying to recall the meeting. "Sorry, I can't..."

"I own that old fishing lodge in Montana. Near Bozeman. Remember?"

"Ah, okay, it's coming back."

"Look, I wonder if you..."

Wyatt squirmed on the chair, setting Cimarron's teeth on edge. Kids made him nervous. In a way, he'd never been a kid himself, and maybe that was why he couldn't seem to identify with them.

"Hold on a minute." Cimarron put his hand over the mouthpiece and turned his attention to the child. "What's your problem? Can't you be still?"

"Gotta go to the bathroom."

Cimarron jerked his head toward a door behind him. "There's one in there. Can you go by yourself?"

The child looked at him as if he had sprouted snakes on his head. "I'm five years old."

"I guess that says it all. Have at it."

"Go ahead," he said to the other man, who launched into a long spiel about his house in a place called Little Lobo.

Listening to the muffled noises behind the bathroom door, Cimarron had to ask Bobby to repeat his words twice. Finally, he gave up. "Let me get back to you. Give me a phone number where I can reach you."

"Okay, but you'd better call pretty soon."

Cimarron jotted down the number, then rolled his chair back and tapped on the door. "What are you doing in there?"

"I'm pooping."

Cimarron rolled his eyes. "Fine." After a moment of guilty hesitation, he asked, "You need any help?"

"No."

Cimarron stuck Bobby James's number on his bulletin board with a note to return his call that afternoon when he could count on being undisturbed. Finally Wyatt came out, careful to close the door behind him.

"Stinks," he said.

"I imagine." Cimarron lifted his chin toward the chair in the corner and Wyatt obediently climbed into the seat again. "Your daddy'll be back in a few minutes."

"Unca Cimron?" Wyatt asked softly. "Do you have something I could draw on?"

Curbing his impatience, Cimarron shuffled around in a drawer and found a legal pad and a pencil, which he handed over. When Wyatt bowed his head over the paper and began to write, Cimarron gathered his thoughts and tried to figure out where he'd left off when his day jumped the tracks.

He studied the costs ledger. This project was almost finished, under budget and on time. Another few weeks, tops, and he could put the house on the market for a substantial asking price. After some time off, he would buy another building that should turn over a good profit after renovation.

He worked uninterrupted while Wyatt occupied himself in the corner. Once in a while Cimarron glanced over, surprised that the child could remain quiet for so long. Wyatt looked up briefly when Cimarron closed the ledger. Then, a commotion outside drew their attention. Another yell from the direction of the house brought Cimarron to his feet. As he opened the trailer door, he saw his project superintendent, Ron Gibbs, sprinting toward him. Beyond Ron, a couple of workmen were rushing into the house.

"What's going on?"

"Accident!" Ron yelled, breathless. "Get an ambulance."

Alarm shot through Cimarron. He grabbed the cordless office phone, punching in 911 as he hurried out the door. On the porch, he turned around to stick his head inside again.

"Wyatt, you stay right here. I'll be back in a few minutes. Understand?"

Without looking up from his drawing, Wyatt nodded.

"What happened?" Cimarron asked when he caught up to Ron.

"Somebody fell."

"Who?"

"I don't know," Ron said. "One of the men came and got me."

The 911 operator answered and Cimarron summoned help, keeping the line open. He matched Ron stride for stride into the stately foyer of the refurbished house. Through the arched entry to the dining room bright sunlight flooded the floor-to-ceiling windows, making the wet paint on the moldings glisten.

Several workers gathered around the base of the high scaffolding that had been erected to reach the twenty-foot ceilings. Cimarron handed the phone to Ron and pushed his way through.

"Oh my God," he whispered, kneeling beside his motionless brother, who was lying faceup on the hardwood floor. "R.J.?"

Cimarron laid his fingers against R.J.'s neck, finding a weak, halting pulse.

"R.J., can you hear me?" He glanced up at the men surrounding him, their faces drawn with concern. "Anybody see what happened?"

A young painter spoke up. "We'd finished and I was getting the brushes and pails ready to go. He was going down to catch them at the bottom. I heard him grunt and when I looked around he was falling. I don't know what happened. Yesterday he was complaining about the fumes making him light-headed and he said living in Louisiana was messing up his sinuses, but he didn't mention anything today. He was just in a big hurry to get done."

R.J.'s eyes fluttered, then opened. He squinted up at Cimarron and managed a lopsided grin. "I must have missed a step," he whispered.

"Just stay still. You'll be okay," Cimarron said with more confidence than he felt.

"Little bro," R.J. said. "You take care of Wyatt, you hear?"

"Come on, R.J., you're going to be around to do that."

"Don't...think...so," he managed to say with effort. Cimarron tried to keep him quiet, but he insisted on speaking. "I made a will...before I came down here. Meant to tell you." He attempted to grin again but failed. "I made you Wyatt's guardian..."

Cimarron stared at his brother in shock. "What?"

"You're the only one I trust...to see that he's done right by. You gotta do it for me, little bro. Give him a good life."

"R.J.—"

R.J.'s eyes rolled back. Cimarron's probing fingers found no pulse this time.

"R.J.!"

No sign of breathing.

"Don't you die on me!"

By rote, Cimarron started CPR, his own heart pounding, drumming out every other sound. Breathe, breathe, pump, pump, pump...

His expression fixed, his face turning blue, R.J. looked just like their mother had when Cimarron turned her over that night so long ago. Sweat poured down his body as the panic grew. He glanced in the direction of the construction office, where a little boy sat waiting...Cimarron would be the one who had to tell him his daddy wasn't coming to get him after all.

No way. No way in hell!

"Damn it, R.J. Don't you die and leave me with that child!"

CHAPTER TWO

LITTLE LOBO, MONTANA
July
OKAY, WHAT DID I DO *to deserve this?*

Sarah James ducked her head to check the big black knobs on the industrial griddle again. All on and set to Medium-High. So why was half of her first pancake crusty brown and the other runny goop? She muttered under her breath and twisted one of the knobs to Off, then back to High, hoping by some miracle the malfunctioning burner would begin to heat.

A customer tapped his menu impatiently on the counter. The pancake was a no-go. She scraped it into the waste bucket that she used to save scraps for a local farmer's pig slop. An apt description, too. Pig slop.

Pushing a damp lock of red hair off her forehead, she turned to the impatient customer. "Sorry. I'll be with you in a moment."

"I ain't got all day, shug," Big Buck Flannigan said. A bull of a man, with a face that was weathered like cowhide, beefy bare arms and a ten-gallon hat perched high on his head, Buck delivered goods from a Bozeman feed distributor to regional hardware stores. He stopped in every few weeks when he came over the pass from Bozeman.

"I know. I'm really sorry. Problems with the griddle."

"I gotta git back on the road. Think you can scrape me up two eggs over easy, order o' linked sausages, some hash browns scattered and slathered, biscuits with gravy and orange juice?"

Sarah jotted down the order, wondering how in the world these foods were going to materialize on her haphazard griddle. Her helper Aaron Dawson would pick a morning when the café was filled to capacity to go AWOL. Sometimes he could make the ancient appliance function when she couldn't. She didn't have time to try to run him down right now, but, boy, when she did find him...

9

She quickly brought Buck's juice and surveyed the room for other impatient customers. Normally she served and Aaron cooked on the large range in the kitchen. She was finding it almost impossible to do both, with the café so crowded. Now she wished she had hired that high-school kid who was looking for a part-time job last week, instead of trying to cut corners and save money.

A stranger opened the door and glanced around until he spotted the only vacant booth left, a table for two tucked into a narrow alcove at the far end of the room. He motioned behind him and a young boy came in. The man lifted the child onto the booth bench, then sat down opposite him. Sarah gave them a cheery "Good morning, be right with you" that she hoped masked her frustration. She noted the resemblance between the two—dark curling hair, striking brown eyes, and the man had a nice smile. But before she could get to them, another customer demanded her attention.

"Look, Miss Sarah, you need to decide if you want me to do the work for you or not. I got other jobs lined up." Harry Upshaw raked his food onto his fork with a piece of biscuit.

He'd been the first to come in this morning and he'd ordered eggs over easy, so that hadn't been too bad. Then half the griddle quit on her, and now she was forced to cook a lot of food on an extremely limited surface. Her only alternative was to cook in the kitchen, but that meant leaving the front and the cash register unattended.

"I do want you to work for me," Sarah said, wishing they could discuss this another time. Like after her customers were gone. "But first we need to sit down and go over the plans and talk about my ideas for the place."

"Now, missy, you know I'll do the job right." He winked. His blue eyes were set in a face roughened and baked by long hours in the sun building houses and running a small cattle operation on the outskirts of town. An ample belly attested to his love of food—he was in the café several times a week.

"I know you will, but I want to be sure that we're on the same track. I have some ideas sketched out and—"

"I don't need no sketches. You just tell me what you want done and I'll make it happen."

"I'll just take the biscuits and gravy now, while I wait," Buck broke in. "I'm goin' to starve here, with you two jabbering."

"Sorry. Hang around just a minute, Harry. I'll be back." At least she could serve biscuits. As always, she had come in early, baked biscuits and brewed urns of coffee using the special house blends that had become her trademark around Little Lobo.

The tiny Montana town just north of the Bozeman Pass made up for its lack of citified entertainment with stunning scenery, wide-open spaces, a tiny school, the basic stores necessary for survival and Sarah's Little Lobo Eatery and Daily Grind. Her special and often exotic coffee and her luscious, fresh-fruit tarts drew regulars from as far away as Big Sky and Helena.

After she served the biscuits, she took a menu and water to the stranger and his little boy. He nodded thanks.

The man was far more handsome than she'd first thought. Black lashes fringed eyes the color of rich Creole coffee and dark, thick hair curled over his forehead, giving him a devil-may-care look that suited his faded jeans and well-worn chambray shirt.

"Do you need some time?" *Please!*

"Sure," he said, opening the menu to study it. From his smile and his glance around, she knew that he realized he was doing her a favor. "Bring a couple of orange juices when you have time."

"No problem." She brought the juice and then made a quick run around the room, refilling water glasses and coffee cups and taking orders from customers who had already been waiting too long.

Ordinarily she would have been overjoyed with the crowd, but today the chatter in the room sounded more like grumbling. Every eye cut her way seemed critical. All she could do was keep smiling and try to get them all fed.

Behind the counter again, trying to cook a dozen things at once on a half-cold griddle, she looked around at Harry. "I want to have Nolan draw up a contract, too. And I still need that estimate I asked for."

Harry downed the last gulp of coffee and ran a pink napkin across his greasy lips, then belched and said, "Puh, contract. We don't need no legalese bull. 'Scuse my language, missy. Anyway, you got a contract with your brother to buy that old house from him?"

Sarah shook her head. "Not yet, just a verbal agreement. But I'm going to pin him down as soon as I can get in touch with him. "

"Didn't think so. Never understood why your uncle Eual split up that property and left the house to Bobby. He shoulda just left everything to you and give Bobby some money to blow. You was the one always spent your summers and holidays here helping him out. Don't recall Bobby so much as lifting a hand in the café *or* the fishing end of the business."

"I think he hoped Bobby would settle down if he had the responsibility of the house. But Little Lobo is too tame for him. He says that house is just a heap of junk and not worth fixing up."

"He ain't far off about the house, I'm afraid. But if you want to try, I'm here to do the job. And you don't need no contract with me, neither. Round here, we don't do business that way. Just give me the go-ahead and 'fore you know it, you'll have a real nice bed-and-breakfast."

Harry shifted a toothpick around in his mouth.

"'Course, I'll need money up front for the initial supplies." He threw a ten on the counter and stood. On his way out he stopped to talk to a couple of townspeople, then left.

"Of course, always the money first," she muttered, rearranging sizzling sausage with another batch of pancakes to try to get them all cooked through. The buzz of conversation behind her began to sound like a hive of angry bees.

She remembered the stranger and his son. Turning around, she found the man watching her. The child colored on a place mat with one of the crayons from a small glass Sarah kept on each table.

"Coming," she said and hurried around the counter to their table. "I'm so sorry for the delays this morning."

"Don't worry about it. He'll take cereal and milk—" the man nodded toward the child, who didn't bother to look up "—I'll have a biscuit with gravy."

"No problem."

He glanced toward the griddle. "Your eggs are burning."

"Oh my gosh! I'll be right back." She raced over to the temperamental griddle, squelching an urge to kick the tar out of it. She doubted that would work and besides she might break a toe. Quickly she put together the order and carried it to the table, laying down the bill at the same time. When she thought to look again a few minutes later, the small booth was empty and payment for the meal rested on the receipt.

· · · ·

IN THE CROWDED parking lot shared by the café and a veterinary clinic next door, Cimarron headed for his truck with Wyatt on his heels. Every step he'd taken for the past month, he'd been dogged by this miniature R.J., like the ghost of his brother constantly reminding him that he'd screwed up. Again. And it was driving Cimarron crazy.

He hoisted Wyatt onto the seat in the cab. "Wait here till I get back."

Wyatt's eyes widened in dread. "Where are you going?"

"Just right up there to look at that house. I won't be gone long. Stay in the truck and don't touch anything."

This morning didn't seem to be the best time to talk to Sarah James, but he could at least look at the old house, which was looming in a forlorn state of disrepair on the hillside behind the café. Square and bulky, three stories high, with dormers and tall chimneys sprouting from a slate roof, the structure's classic bones had been altered over the years by clumsy additions to the sides and a utilitarian porch that hid the crafts-manship of the original molding around the front entrance. The front door stood open, beckoning Cimarron to explore.

"I want to go, too," Wyatt said, his eyes and voice pleading. He hadn't liked to be alone for a minute since his daddy died.

An occasional car passed on the two-lane highway leading out of town, the drone of tires on asphalt rising and then ebbing away to noth-ing as each vehicle disappeared around the bend. Cimarron hesitated with his hand on the door of his truck. Finally, he exhaled hard and put the kid back on the ground again. "Just don't get in my way and don't touch anything."

"Okay."

Always *okay*. Never any protest unless Cimarron tried to get out of his sight for two seconds.

Cimarron shook his head and strode off, with Wyatt right behind. When he entered the musty-smelling parlor, a rush of images came to him, some faded, with tattered edges like old photographs long mis-placed. This place had been a fishing lodge in its prime and Cimarron could imagine the boom of laughter as fishermen warmed themselves with whiskey and a roaring fire and told tall tales of their day in the stream.

With a practiced eye, Cimarron assessed the condition of the once-proud room, which had deteriorated over time into a shadowy dust-covered ruin. The bad news? Rotting ledges at the bottom of two of the tall windows facing the mountains; holes in the plaster; dry, splin-tered floorboards that creaked under his weight as he crossed the room. The good news? The house had good bones and the problems Cimar-ron noticed at first glance appeared to be only superficial. He ran his hand appreciatively along the intricately carved mantel over the parlor fireplace before climbing the elegant staircase to inspect each of the six bedrooms and a miscellany of smaller rooms. Wyatt stuck to him like a shadow, but he'd given up trying to pry the child away weeks ago. Easier to just keep him pacified for the time being.

Downstairs once more, he pulled a small pad and pencil from his pocket and sat on a windowsill in the parlor to jot down his thoughts and make note of a few measurements he'd taken. The morning sun warmed his back through the rippled glass panes. He was in no hurry to leave and had nowhere to go.

• • • •

CROWDING EVERYTHING on the hot side of the griddle, Sarah managed to finish the morning cooking without losing her mind. An hour and a half later, the last table cleared as a tourist family of four that had run her ragged finally left. At least her regular customers had understood her dilemma and been patient with the poor service, so she'd cut a percentage off each ticket, even though she needed every penny of income. As soon as the front door clicked shut, she grabbed the phone and called Aaron's cell number. No answer. Furious now, she punched in another number and drummed her fingers on the counter waiting for an answer.

"Hello?" she said in surprise when a woman answered. "I'm trying to reach Aaron. He didn't show up for work today."

"I know, Miss Sarah." The woman's voice wavered. "I'm his mother, Martha, and I just got home. He's so sick he can hardly lift his head off the pillow. He only managed to call me a few minutes ago."

"Oh, I see." Sarah's anger waned. "Does he need a doctor?" She didn't know the family very well, only that Aaron worked and saved most of his money by living at home.

"I think it's just a stomach bug, but if he's not better tomorrow he won't be in."

"I understand. Please have him call me when he feels better to let me know when he'll be back."

"I will. He really likes that job, so I know he'll be there as soon as he can."

Sarah settled the phone into place on the wall cradle and leaned against the counter for a weary moment before tackling the messy tables. She filled a large garbage bag and hauled it out the back door to the Dumpster. Glancing up, she noticed movement in her uncle's old house on the hill. She shaded her eyes against the bright sunshine and frowned. Somebody was definitely sitting in the window. Who was on her property and why?

Several vehicles were parked at her best friend Kaycee Rider's veterinary clinic next door, but on this side a lone black extended-cab pickup with a fancy camper shell sat in the parking lot. She glanced at the magnetic sign on the door, which sported a colorful "house" logo with the scrolled letters VRR intertwined and overlaid on a red C. Below that Vision Restoration and Renovation and an out-of-state phone number appeared.

Some consultant Harry had called in? He hadn't mentioned any outside firm to her. She started up the hill, noticing Kaycee and an assistant in the corral behind the clinic working with a lame horse.

Quietly she went through the open door. *Lock it next time.* From the arched doorway between the entrance hall and the main parlor, she could see the stranger who'd eaten in the café sitting in the bay window, his dark head bent over the tablet on his knee as he wrote.

"Excuse me," Sarah said.

He looked up and shot her a heart-stopping smile. "I see you survived the breakfast crowd."

"What are you doing in here?" she demanded.

"Interesting house," he said, rising.

"This is private property. Are you working with Harry Upshaw?"

The little boy beside him stopped playing with the toy in his hand. He looked up at Sarah with big brown eyes and crept behind the man's legs, peeking around at her.

"Was that the contractor you were talking to in the café?"

"Yes, he's going to start working on the house next week."

"Nope. I don't work with anybody."

"Then what are you doing in here? Did it occur to you to ask permission before you trespassed?"

"You were somewhat rushed this morning." He tucked his pad and pencil into his shirt pocket. "It's a beautiful old house."

Sarah stared at him. "You're the first person who's said that in a long time."

"Obviously well built. Just a bit run-down. Most of the problems are cosmetic."

"I'm glad to hear that. I'm going to remodel it and turn it into a bed-and-breakfast."

"Remodel? This house deserves to be restored."

"Love to, but I can't afford it."

His lips pressed together and his brow knitted.

"That's too bad."

"Why?"

"I'd hate to see a fine old mansion like this messed up any more than it already has been. The craftsmanship is irreplaceable."

"What business is this of yours?"

He blew out a long breath, rubbed his hand across his mouth and said, "It belongs to me now. Your brother Bobby sold it to me."

CHAPTER THREE

SARAH SUCKED IN a shocked breath. She clamped her fists against her hips and glared at him. He hoped she wasn't the fainting kind.

"That's a lie!" she snapped, alleviating his worry that she might swoon. But the nearly imperceptible tremor in her chin belied her bravado.

He almost smiled at her pretty face, which was suddenly as pale as porcelain except for a sprinkling of freckles across her cheeks. Her turquoise eyes were shooting sparks.

"No, ma'am, it's not. I've got the documents in my truck, if you want to look them ov—"

She gave an adamant shake of her head, unleashing several red curls that immediately fell across her forehead. Brusquely she shoved them back. "I don't care what papers you've got. Bobby can't sell this property to you."

"Why?"

"Because I'm buying it from him."

"You've got a legal document to that effect?" Cimarron asked, recalling the earlier conversation he'd overheard between her and the local contractor.

Wyatt's hands squeezed Cimarron's leg in a death grip. He fought the urge to shake the boy off so he could concentrate. Sarah hesitated for a second, lips pressed tight.

"No, not exactly."

"Not exactly?"

"We have a verbal agreement. It's always been understood that he would sell the house to me."

"An 'understanding' is not going to hold water. I've got a legal bill of sale."

He considered ducking to avoid the daggers being thrown from her eyes.

"I don't care. Your papers aren't worth a plug nickel. A verbal agreement is binding, too. Bobby can give you the money back and the deal's off."

That underhanded brother of hers hadn't told Cimarron that anybody else wanted the place. In fact, he'd never mentioned a sister at all. He'd acted like the house was his, free and clear.

"It's not that easy."

"Why?"

"Couple of reasons. For one thing, did it occur to you I might not want to negate the deal? I've got plans for this house."

She narrowed her eyes. "What plans? Who are you anyway, and how do you know my brother? Why do you want my house?"

"Cimarron Cole. I met your brother last year in New Orleans and he told me about the house. I had a friend check the place out, and I made an offer. Bobby turned me down back then, but he called a few weeks ago to see if I was still interested. It seemed like a good investment...at the time."

"How could he do this to me?" Bewilderment clouded her face for a moment, then she clenched her jaw and straightened her back. "And how did somebody check out my house without my permission?"

"Don't guess he realized he needed permission. Bobby said the house was his, which I get the feeling is the truth. Maybe you were busy in the café and didn't notice. I doubt he'd have been here long."

"It doesn't matter, Bobby and I had a verbal agreement and I want my house back. Just let me find him and make him return your money."

"Good luck," he said with a smirk.

"What do you mean by that?"

Cimarron gently disengaged Wyatt from his leg. "Go over there and play," he said. Wyatt hesitated, still leery of the stranger. "Go, I said." Cimarron gave the boy a slight push and Wyatt reluctantly crossed the floor to sit on the edge of the hearth, ready to bolt back at a moment's notice.

Cimarron leaned against the window frame and crossed his arms. "The last time I saw your brother, the taillights of his brand-new Coachman RV were disappearing around the bend, and his new show-girl-turned-bride was waving her bejeweled hand out the window. I doubt the ink was dry on the sales contract."

"What? He got married? Again?" Her exasperated voice rose to a squeak. "A Coachman? Isn't that the big..."

Cimarron nodded. "Yep. About a hundred thousand dollars big. And the wedding rings were probably another fifteen grand."

He thought the woman was going to faint for sure this time. Her hand flew to her throat and her mouth fell open. "How much did you pay?"

"A hell of a lot more than I would have if I'd known the real situation. But the fact is, Bobby's already run through most of it and I don't think you're going to be seeing him for a while."

She sank to the windowsill. "I don't have that kind of money," she whispered.

"I don't want your money anyway. I want the house. Bobby never mentioned your interest in it."

"He's such a rotten brother," she said.

Cimarron agreed, but held his tongue.

"This property has been in our family for generations. Bobby promised he'd sell his part to me."

"I believe dear Bobby went for the bucks, not family loyalty. If I hadn't bought it, his plan was to move on to the next bidder."

She surprised him by muttering, "The little shit." Then she looked up with bold determination. "I'll get the money to buy it back. I'll get a loan."

"No bank's going to loan you the amount I paid for this house. Not the way it looks right now."

"I thought you said it was in good enough shape."

"It is, but not to the casual eye."

"I'll get an appraiser."

"It won't appraise for what I intend to sell it for. Besides, you'd spend the rest of your life paying back that kind of loan, even with a bed-and-breakfast."

"I don't care." She faced him squarely, her eyes glinting fire. "You're not going to get it. I'll sue you."

"For what? It's a binding bill of sale. We'll be tied up in legal red tape for years. Can you afford that expense?"

"That's my business."

"Okay. But it'll be a waste of time and money for both of us."

"It's not fair!"

Cimarron didn't like the heaviness that had settled in his midsection. He hadn't anticipated this stumbling block when he bought the old house, but he was pretty sure Sarah James couldn't buy the place back at his price and he wasn't about to lose money on the deal. "It's life. And I won't lose."

"We'll see about that," she retorted and stalked over to the door. She turned back in the entryway. "You and your son can leave now. I'm locking the door."

"Fine," Cimarron said and motioned to Wyatt, who came to heel like a puppy and followed him outside. He didn't mention the fact that Bobby had given him a set of keys to the house. No need to provoke her more.

At the truck, Wyatt slid into the backseat and Cimarron moved behind the wheel, then sat for a while with the door open, a boot propped on the dashboard, pondering his options. He'd never get any money back from Bobby. Sarah might risk everything she had to regain the house and Cimarron would have to add that guilt to the bundle that already weighed him down. Yet he couldn't just throw his money to the wind. He'd intended to start work on this place right away, while he figured out what to do about Wyatt.

He thought about Sarah working so hard in the café that morning and recalled that her griddle was broken. They would never work things out as enemies. If he had to make a conciliatory move, so be it. He was a businessman and every day of lost work meant lost money.

Busy printing a lunch and dinner menu on the large chalkboard behind the counter, Sarah purposefully ignored Cimarron when he came into the café again. Without help and with only one side of her griddle working, she would be hard-pressed to handle more than a few simple items today.

To her advantage, Saturdays in Little Lobo were usually slow. Working people took off to Livingston or Bozeman to shop and restock groceries. Ranchers and farmers had to catch up while they could. Usually, after breakfast no more than a dozen folks stopped by the café on a given Saturday. She planned to serve cold sandwiches and a big pot of soup. Even without Aaron, she could manage that.

Cimarron waited in silence for her to finish.

She laid her colored chalk in the tray at the bottom of the board and turned to face him. "What do you want?"

"Is your griddle working now?"

"No."

"I could probably fix it for you."

"Jack-of-all-trades," she said with an edge of sarcasm that could have sliced beef. "I didn't ask for your help."

"I'm offering."

"No, thanks."

His jaw hardened and a fist clenched, but he maintained his stoic composure. "I didn't intend to mess up your plans when I came here."

"You could have fooled me."

"It's not me you should be mad with. Your brother's the one who misled us both."

"Oh, trust me, I'm mad with him. I just can't get my hands on him right this minute."

"That doesn't bode well for me." He shot her a disarming grin that revealed beautiful white teeth and warmed his eyes.

His charm almost worked. Almost. Sarah wasn't going to be sucked in by a handsome face. "No, it doesn't. So why don't you leave?"

"We're never going to come to an agreement if we can't even talk."

"There won't be an agreement. You and Bobby cheated me, and I'm going to rectify that."

"I didn't cheat you. Long story short, I can't afford to lose my money and you can't afford to pay me back, so we're going to have to work something out. In the meantime, let me look at your griddle before you open for lunch."

"I don't need it for lunch, but..." Grudgingly she gave a curt nod.

She moved out of his way as he came around the counter. At least that would be one thing she wouldn't have to worry about. He fiddled with the griddle controls, then inched the heavy unit away from the wall.

"Where's your little boy?"

"Wyatt?" He glanced at his knee. "You mean he's not attached to my leg?"

She looked around for the child, noticing a small foot sticking out of one of the booths. The child was lying on his stomach on the bench, his head resting on his arm.

"Do you want something to drink?" she asked him.

"He'll be fine," Cimarron said as Wyatt lifted his head to look at her. He put his head back down and said nothing.

Sarah frowned. "I don't mind giving him—"

"Do you have any tools in here. If not, I've got mine in the truck."

None of my business. She pulled a worn leather tool pouch from under the counter. Cimarron chose a screwdriver and took the back off the unit.

"Here's the problem," he said. "One of your burners is shot."

"So you can't fix it?"

"Not without a new part. Any appliance-repair places around here?"

"Bozeman," she said glumly.

"Okay. I'll drive into Bozeman and try to find a replacement."

"That's too much trouble."

"Do you have any other options?"

Sarah gave that some serious thought. Seemed she was fresh out of options on all sides.

"Not at the moment. I called around and the local repairman is out of town for several days. Of course, nobody from Bozeman will come this far out without adding a surcharge—and never on a weekend."

"Then I'll be back as soon as I can."

"I...I'd rather you didn't. I don't want to owe you any favors."

"The only thing I ask in return is that you quit skewering me for something your brother did. Let's see how things look in the morning. Can you just do that?"

Still in shock, and with two more meals to serve before she could rest, Sarah was in no mood to capitulate. But if this stranger wanted to fix her griddle, let him.

"I'll pay you to fix it, but your stealing my house still won't look any different to me tomorrow."

CHAPTER FOUR

THE AIR WAS COOL and clear at the top of Bozeman Pass and the unrelenting wind whipped through Cimarron's open truck windows as he enjoyed the panorama spread before him. This part of Montana called to his heart, even more than his native Idaho.

Why return to a place that triggered unhappy memories of the medicinal smells, sickbeds, and the depression and hopelessness of watching one parent die while the other spiraled into a void of alcohol and irresponsibility? Where roots no longer existed, except in the lonely country graveyard where his brother was now buried next to their mother. His only remaining family—that he was willing to claim, anyway—was firmly planted in the backseat of the pickup as they barreled along.

Cimarron hadn't expected the determined challenge from Sarah James, but he stood a good chance of wearing her down—especially since he suspected she didn't have the money to put up a convincing fight. He'd just have to hang around until everything was resolved.

That had a definite upside. Cimarron arched an eyebrow and smiled. Even at her maddest, she was cute as a speckled puppy, with her shining red hair, flaming cheeks and eyes the color of an endless sky.

Maybe everything would actually work out. Unless she managed to destroy the big house while he was gone. Not a good thought. He barely knew the woman, and judging by her brother's character, anything was possible. He pushed the speedometer up a notch. She could burn his place to the ground by the time he made the round-trip to Bozeman.

"Unca Cimron, are we gonna live in that house?"

Cimarron glanced at Wyatt, then back at the highway. Buckled into a booster seat, Wyatt rotated his toy truck in his hands, pretending to study it.

"Maybe for a while. Why?"

A small shoulder shrugged. "Don't look very nice."

"Well, I plan to fix it up."

"Oh. Do you have a house somewhere else for us to live?"

"No. I don't have a house. I live in this truck. And sometimes I live in a trailer, when I'm working on a house."

"Can we live in a trailer while you work on that house?"

"Might be fun to live in the house. We can pretend we're camping out."

"That lady said no."

"That lady doesn't know everything."

"It's kinda spooky. That old house..."

"You scared?" In the rearview mirror, Cimarron caught a glimpse of Wyatt's lower lip trembling. "Come on, you're a big boy. Besides, it's just old. Nothing in there to be scared of. Anyway, we won't be here that long."

Wyatt brightened. "Okay."

"Listen, Wyatt..." Cimarron licked his dry lips. "There's something I've been meaning to talk to you about."

"Okay."

"Do you think you'd be happier living with somebody besides me? I mean, I'm on the road all the time and..."

"My daddy," Wyatt said softly. "That's all."

"Yeah, I understand. But you know how that is. I was just wondering..." Cimarron let the words trail off as his palms grew sweaty on the steering wheel. Sooner or later, he had to tell Wyatt about his plans, but somehow he chickened out every time he tried to explain. He had no business scoffing at Wyatt for being afraid of a spooky old house. He was completely frightened by a five-year-old. Not to mention his brother's ghost.

"I don't want to live with nobody else."

Cimarron pulled into the parking lot of a large home-improvement store, hoping to find the part he needed. Three stores later, he found a replacement burner and they headed toward Little Lobo once more. Cimarron breathed a sigh of relief when he pulled into the parking lot. The house was still standing.

He took the new burner and the tools required from the back of his truck. Sarah was nowhere to be found, but the rear door to the café stood open and the screen was unlatched. The place was spotless. Apparently she'd made it through lunch. Cimarron put Wyatt in the booth with his backpack of toys and went behind the counter to work.

Sarah came in the kitchen door a few minutes later and busied herself there while he continued to work in the dining area. Half an hour later, he wiped the last trace of grease from the stainless griddle. He walked into the other room to clean his hands.

Chopping an onion with a vengeance on a cutting board near the double sinks, Sarah didn't look up. Through the windows the disputed house loomed, a reminder of the reason for the tension hovering in the room.

"Your griddle's fixed."

Silence.

A to-do list hung on the corkboard above the counter.

Chop onions

Soup base

Fry bacon

Slice tomatoes

Peel boiled eggs

Ice in front bin

Slice deli meat

Brew fresh coffee

Cimarron stopped reading and put a large skillet on the stove. Adjusting the heat, he rummaged in the refrigerator until he found a butcher-paper packet marked Bacon. He laid the strips side by side until the bottom of the pan was covered, the only sound in the room that of the meat beginning to sizzle and the *rat-a-tat-tat* of Sarah's chopping. Sarah cut her eyes around at him.

"I don't want your help," she said.

"I know you don't. But you need it." He turned the crisping bacon with tongs taken from overhead hooks that were laden with a conglomeration of kitchen tools. A larger rack hung nearby, loaded with industrial pots and pans.

While the bacon continued to cook, Cimarron peeled one after another of the boiled brown eggs that were sitting in a bowl on the counter. Sarah scooped her chopped onions into a container, popped the top on it and began to slice the bloodred tomatoes nestled in a colander set in the sink.

The comforting smell of bacon filled the room, making it hard to hold a grudge.

"Thanks," she said softly. "For the griddle...and this..."

"I don't see how you do it alone."

"I usually have help. He's sick."

"Just two of you?"

"Yes. Bobby used to help out, but—" She laid the sliced tomatoes in a container, then diced the rest. "You're pretty good at this."

"Lots of practice when I was young."

"I see. Why?"

Cimarron busied himself moving the bacon to a paper towel–lined pan. "Do you want this bacon whole or crumbled for the salad?"

"A third of it whole, the rest for the salad." She turned and leaned against the counter, her eyes on him as she dried her hands on a towel. "You're not going to answer me, are you?"

He met her clear gaze straight on. "Nope."

"Why are you helping me like this? To bribe me?"

"No. I don't work that way."

"How do you work, Mr. Cole? How did you talk my brother into selling out to you without so much as a word to me?"

Cimarron almost told her the truth, but then he bit back the words. She probably loved her brother, even though right now she'd never admit it. No need to paint her a picture of the louse Bobby really was. He shook his head and went back to his task with the bacon.

"What? Did you get him drunk? Or just keep offering him more money until he couldn't resist?" Lingering fury smoldered in her words. "Have you been after him for a long time? Until finally you wore him down?"

She dumped stock and sautéed vegetables into a tall soup pot, seasoned the mixture and put a lid on to let it simmer.

"I think you're a cheat."

"Well, I'm not. I didn't cheat your brother out of anything. Have you located him yet?"

"No."

"Not likely to, either," Cimarron muttered.

Sarah huffed, but backed off. "Where's your little boy now?"

"Playing in a booth."

"He's very quiet. Most kids that age make a lot more racket. What's his name?"

"Name's Wyatt. Don't worry about him, he's fine."

The bell over the front door tinkled and Sarah threw the towel aside, smoothing her hair back.

"Thanks for helping. Do you want to feed Wyatt before you go?"

"I'm not going anywhere."

"No, really, I'll get by tonight. There's no need for you to stay. If you'll leave your name and a way to get in touch, I'll have my lawyer contact you to straighten this out."

Cimarron shook his head, amazed at her stubbornness.

"You won't have a problem there. We're going to sleep in the house."

"You are not! I won't let you in."

Cimarron reached in his pocket and brought out the key ring, dangling it in front of her. "Why would I buy a house and not get the keys for it?"

She stiffened and stared at the jingling keys. "Ooh, I'm going to kill Bobby."

"I'd better get Wyatt out of your way."

"Wyatt is not the one who's in my way. And we'll deal with this later."

Cimarron followed her as she pushed through the swinging doors and went to greet the first dinner customers. He motioned for Wyatt, and the child came obediently through the kitchen door. Cimarron had a look through the cupboards and coolers until he found some sliced turkey and bread. He made Wyatt a sandwich and found a safe corner for him to play away from the kitchen appliances.

"Sorry, bud, you're on your own for the rest of the evening."

Wyatt settled down with his backpack at his side and took the sandwich and glass of milk Cimarron offered. "Okay."

Enough with the *okays!* Maybe one day the kid would learn another word.

Cimarron continued to work in the kitchen, doing most of the cooking according to Sarah's clipped directions while she waited tables through the next three chaotic hours. He wiped his brow with a shirt-sleeve and sweat trickled down his back, the heat of the kitchen intensified by Sarah's anger. He held on to his own temper by the thinnest thread. No place for a blowup between them, with a café full of customers who would have very long memories and very loose tongues, if Cimarron's recollection of small-town life held true.

When all was quiet and the last customer had paid and left, he let out a long sigh as he heard Sarah click the lock on the front door. He was whipped, tired to the bone, just as he was at the end of every long day since his brother died. The feeling was nothing like the exhausted satisfaction of hard physical labor on a house. Not at all. He could leave now and let Sarah finish on her own but knowing she would be stuck working for hours if he did, he started scrubbing the pots and pans.

• • • •

S ARAH PAUSED in her cleanup of the dining room to cock an ear toward the kitchen. In there, Cimarron whistled softly amidst the clatter of metal as he washed dishes. He had worked like a Trojan tonight and now he was cleaning the kitchen yet anger still roiled inside her. She didn't want him doing anything else thoughtful to make her feel guilty.

She knew she was taking out her frustration with her brother on Cimarron, but she couldn't help it. All her dreams, her plans, her future income had been blown to pieces by her brother's greed. Cimarron seemed like a nice enough guy, but under the circumstances he could be a saint and she'd still feel the same way. She wanted her property back.

She rolled the cleanup cart to the doorway. "You can go now. I'll finish up."

"Most everything's done in here, anyway."

The pans sat on the drainboard, shining clean, the counters had all been wiped down. Damp dishcloths waited in the laundry basket in the corner. Unused food had been put away. All Sarah had to do was load the dishwasher and start the linens washing.

"Wow...thanks," she said, wishing she liked him better. He'd saved her a ton of work. "I...I can handle breakfast myself in the morning. That's the only meal I serve on Sundays."

He nodded. "All right."

"There's a little motel a few miles down the road." She hoped he'd take the hint.

"I know. I saw it on the way to Bozeman."

"So, you can stay there."

"I think not. I don't have to pay to stay in my own house."

"We'll see how long that lasts." She jerked open the door to load the dishwasher, then straightened and looked around. "Where's Wyatt?"

Cimarron turned to a corner of the kitchen, started to speak, then paled when he saw the cubbyhole was empty. "He was right there."

"Maybe he slipped out the back door."

"I would have heard him. He's here somewhere. Wyatt?" Cimarron moved to the area where Wyatt's toys were still strewn about. He squatted and let out a breath of relief. "Here he is."

Sarah followed Cimarron's gaze. The child was curled into a ball on an open shelf under the counter, all but hidden from view. Cimarron stuffed the toys into the bag and gently slid Wyatt out. He hoisted the bag by its strap over one shoulder and lifted the boy over the opposite.

Sarah studied the two of them. Neither was at ease and she wondered why. Newsreels of kidnapped children ran through her mind. True these two looked just alike, but family abductions happened all the time.

"You're not very good at looking after him, are you?" she said bluntly.

"I knew where he was."

Sarah shook her head. "I saw that look of panic. You'd forgotten about him. Didn't have a clue if he was still in the room."

To her surprise, he didn't argue. "I'm going to put him to bed now."

"In that dirty old house?"

"We'll sleep another night in the back of the camper." Cimarron lowered his voice as Wyatt shifted and mumbled something. "You and I will talk tomorrow about the house."

The screen door slammed after him and Sarah was left alone and thoroughly dispirited. When all the closing chores were done, she did a final circuit of the café, double-checked the locked doors and climbed the stairs to her apartment. She loved living above the café for convenience, but she was looking forward to having more space when she moved into the bed-and-breakfast—a prospect now put on hold because of her double-crossing brother.

Although the café was decorated in pink, she'd chosen an array of other colors for her personal quarters—sunny yellow for the spacious living room and kitchen, and peaceful celadon green for the bedroom. Casual furnishings and a minimum of clutter made the apartment a perfect retreat after long hours in the café.

She opened a window and let the cool air and soothing night noises calm her nerves as she looked down on the parking lot. Cimarron's truck, dark inside, was parked at the back. Hoping it would be gone in the morning, she began to get ready for bed. But she was pretty sure her worst nightmare would still be around when the sun came up.

CHAPTER FIVE

THE CUSTOM CAMPER shell on the back of Cimarron's pickup was outfitted with bare-bones necessities assembled to suit Cimarron's vagabond lifestyle, but there was little space for an extra person—even one as small as Wyatt. His presence in the cramped space made Cimarron almost claustrophobic.

Cimarron settled Wyatt into the camouflage sleeping bag they'd bought after R.J.'s death. Wyatt considered sleeping on the floor of the camper "adventure sleeping." Cimarron just considered it inconvenient. He had been stepping over and on toys, small articles of clothing and Wyatt for weeks, and he was at his wit's end to find a minute of privacy in order to regroup and try to figure out a solution. He'd intended to stay in the house just to have a bit of room to move around, but Sarah's stubborn resistance might make that difficult.

When Wyatt's even breathing assured him the child was asleep, he slipped outside for some fresh air. The dark night was tempered by a half moon and also the warm glow of Sarah's security light on a pole in the parking lot. Cimarron paced the lot for a few minutes to work off his tension.

What the hell was he going to do with this child? How could he raise Wyatt and give him a decent life? But there was nobody else to take him. Cimarron had no idea where his no-account father might be—dead or alive. Even if he was alive, he'd never get his hands on Wyatt, considering the childhood he'd inflicted on Cimarron.

R.J. hadn't talked much about what had happened with Wyatt's birth mother, Joy, but Cimarron got the idea that R.J. hadn't been the only bull in the pasture and Joy hadn't had the ability or inclination to take proper care of a baby. She signed over her parental rights to R.J. soon after Wyatt was born. Re-married now, she'd made it clear when Cimarron called to tell her about R.J.'s death that she had no intention of claiming her son. Hell, she hadn't even told her new husband she had an illegitimate child. There was no denying Wyatt's paternity, however, and that left Cimarron stuck with the total responsibility of a family member—again. He muttered under his breath and kicked the light pole as he passed. Stupid move. He hobbled the rest of the way to the truck, choking back curses. About his foot, his fate, his future. Just wasn't right. He hadn't fathered that kid, and he didn't want any more responsibility for other people. He hadn't done a good job before, and he had no reason to believe he'd fare any better with Wyatt.

Sitting down on the broad bumper of his truck, he leaned back against the camper and closed his eyes, trying to allay the coil of panic that squirmed in his gut every time the undeniable truth hit him. His life would never be the same again.

Cimarron opened his eyes at the sound of a vehicle turning into the parking lot. He squinted as a blinding spotlight flared to life, pointing directly at him. Red and blue lights reflected off the nearby buildings and his pickup.

"What the hell?" he muttered, throwing a hand up to shield his eyes.

"Don't move. Keep your hands up where I can see them!"

A sheriff's deputy eased toward Cimarron with one hand on his sidearm, the other moving a powerful flashlight around.

Cimarron raised his hands, turning his head to the side and grimacing at the bright lights. At least the deputy hadn't drawn on him—yet. Cimarron glanced up at the window above the café and saw Sarah staring down. *Damn it, did she call the cops on me?* The deputy caught his attention again, moving enough to one side that Cimarron could turn away from the spotlight to face him.

"What are you doing here this time of night? The café's been closed for hours," he said. "Let me see some ID."

"I'm sleeping in my truck. Sarah knows I'm here."

"Yeah, sure she does. Now get behind the wheel of that truck and get moving, or I'll give you a different option for a few nights."

"Look, Deputy—" Cimarron eyed the deputy's badge "—Whitman, I don't want any trouble." He slowly lowered his hands. "I've got a right to be here."

"That ID?"

"It's in my wallet." Cimarron reached for his back pocket.

"Easy now, *real* slow," Deputy Whitman said.

Cimarron withdrew his wallet and fished out his driver's license.

"I bought that house. I have a right to be here."

The deputy guffawed. "I know who owns this land, mister. And it ain't you."

"I've got the paperwork. Can I get it to show you?"

"Where is it?"

"Front seat of my truck."

The deputy moved with Cimarron to the side of the truck. Cimarron opened the door and pointed to the folder lying on the console. He'd intended to show it to Sarah, but he'd never gotten the chance.

"Just have a look at the paperwork. I own the house and the property around it." He pulled out the title and handed it over.

The deputy shined the light on the paper and checked the signature at the bottom. "Well, that sure looks like Bobby's signature. Lord knows I've seen it enough on traffic tickets. But it might be forged."

"It's not forged."

"Come around to the front of my car while I check this out."

The deputy took the folder and Cimarron's license with him and called in the information. Cimarron leaned against the fender of the patrol car, arms crossed, staring up at Sarah's now-empty window, stewing over the possibility that she was responsible for him being on the brink of going to jail. A light came on downstairs a few moments later. If she'd reported him, there would be no more Mr. Nice Guy—and no more kitchen boy, for sure.

"Well, you checked out okay. But I'm not happy with you hanging around here. Find yourself somewhere else to stay."

Cimarron rolled his eyes. "Give me a break. Sarah knows I'm here and I don't see why I have to leave. Especially since—"

"Hey, Griff," Sarah said, coming across the parking lot in silky long pajamas and a robe. Sexy as hell, with her hair down and brushed to a satin sheen. The pale green color of the pajamas complemented her freshly scrubbed face.

"Hey, Sarah. Sorry to disturb you," Deputy Whitman said.

"No, that's okay." She eyed Cimarron. "I'm glad you're looking out for me."

Cimarron lifted an eyebrow and shot her a wry look. Probably everybody in this one-horse town was protective of her.

"He's got some kinda paperwork here, says he bought out your brother Bobby."

Sarah glanced at the paper and frowned. "Yes, I know. But I'm contacting my lawyer first thing Monday morning to see if it's legal."

"It's legal," Cimarron said.

Both of them ignored him.

"Do you want me to take him in?"

"Now, wait a minute..."

"No," Sarah said quickly. "I told him he could stay here for the night. Bobby sort of tricked him into buying the property. I'm sure I'll get it straightened out next week."

Deputy Whitman looked dubious as he handed back the paperwork. "I don't like it. And I'm going to see that you're locked in before I leave."

"Really, Griff, there's no need for that. Like I said..."

"Either I make sure you're safe for the night, or I lock him up."

"On what charge?" Cimarron demanded.

"I'll think of something," Deputy Whitman growled.

This was more than professional concern for Sarah. Cimarron sensed a strong undercurrent of male competitiveness in the deputy. Did he have an eye for the lovely Miss James? Cimarron couldn't blame him, but that wasn't grounds for arrest.

She held up her hands in appeasement. "Stop this. See me to the door if it makes you feel better, Griff."

The deputy handed Cimarron his license and paperwork. "You find a better place to camp after tonight. And trust me, I'll be back by here a few times before morning." He guided Sarah toward the café.

Cimarron returned to his truck but stopped short of getting in, curious to see what move Deputy Whitman might put on Sarah. She quickly disappeared inside, however, leaving the officer standing on the stoop. He waited a moment longer and Cimarron took that opportunity to climb into the camper and close the door.

• • • •

THE NEXT MORNING, Cimarron rose early. Wanting to avoid another visit by the overzealous law officer, he moved his truck behind the mansion out of sight of the road. Since Sarah had made it clear she didn't want any help in the café this morning, he pulled out fishing gear, packed a lunch for two, then got Wyatt up and moving. He'd wait until the café closed to clear out a spot to live in the old house. Maybe Sarah would go visiting this afternoon and he could work in peace.

Finding a map for the house and surrounding property among his paperwork, he located the trout stream that Bobby had mentioned. According to the surveyor's markings, Cimarron's two hundred acres adjoined Sarah's much larger holding halfway between the house and café. The property narrowed to about seven hundred feet of road frontage, more than enough for access to both buildings, and then spread out like a fan across the valley and the lower reaches of the closest mountain. On the map, a broad tributary of the Little Lobo River meandered diagonally through both pieces of property, and Bobby had sworn it was teeming with trout. Bobby's credibility had taken a dive since he'd given Cimarron that map, but just casting a rod could relieve a world of tension.

Wyatt was a trouper, Cimarron had to give him that. In his worn cowboy boots and the black cowboy hat that his daddy had given him, the boy trudged through the underbrush without complaint, even when Cimarron had to extricate him from the thorny clutches of a bramble bush.

The dense woods suddenly opened onto a sweep of sun-bejeweled water rushing by a grassy expanse of bank. Jutting boulders split the pristine current, and the hope of silver-sided trout in the deep pools lifted Cimarron's spirits. The soft touch of the rising sun warmed his face. The scent of evergreens hung heavy on the morning air and the murmur of the water was the only sound to be heard. This was as close to heaven as Cimarron ever expected to get.

"Unca Cimron?"

Zap! The euphoria vanished.

"What?"

"Are we going to fish now?"

"I'm going to fish. You're going to sit on the bank and eat your breakfast."

Cimarron pulled a sandwich from his gear bag along with a bottled orange juice and handed them both to Wyatt. He'd confiscated the sandwich fixings from Sarah's kitchen the evening before and stashed them overnight in the ice chest in the camper.

"I can fish," Wyatt insisted.

"I don't have another rod. Now sit there and be quiet. You'll scare the fish off."

Wyatt took the food and sat on the bank to eat, an unhappy scowl on his face. To access the items in his bag, Cimarron took out the other two sandwiches, tucked them into his jacket pocket and laid the jacket across a low bush, then pulled on a pair of stocking-feet waders and lightweight folding boots. From a hard cylindrical case, he removed a custom Winston fly rod with his name lettered in gold on the side. He'd done a modest reconstruction on a cottage that belonged to one of the managers of the company and had taken part of his fee in fishing equipment. Light and agile, the rod never failed to amaze him.

He rigged the rod and reel under Wyatt's watchful eye, then fixed a tiny fly with a pinched-down hook to the tippet at the end of the leader and tightened the knot with his teeth. Rather than kicking the bushes himself to see what the trout delicacy of the week might be, he'd checked in Bozeman the day before for the current hatch and bought suitable flies and a fishing license.

Striding into the cold water, he flicked the rod back and forth, letting out line with a smooth, graceful motion. He allowed the fly to settle for a moment on the calm surface of a deep pool behind an outcropping of rocks, hoping for a rise to the bait.

He had spent a lot of hours like this as a youth, fishing a favorite stream near his home, escaping his burdens for a few hours at a time. Nature was better than any therapy.

When the fly floated downstream, he cast again and placed the fly once more. Once in a while, R.J. would fish with him, on the rare and brief occasions when he and their father came home. As much as he resented their inevitable abandonment, Cimarron always enjoyed spending time with his brother. R.J. could usually outfish him, but it didn't matter by the time they got home and fried the succulent trout. Today Cimarron missed his brother's camaraderie more than ever. He tried to get his mind off R.J. and everything else that had dragged at his heart lately.

A trout rose to his fly but didn't bite. Patiently mending his lie closer to the rocks, Cimarron watched the concentric circles disturb the pool's smooth surface.

Like the ripple effects of his brother's death. Complications Cimarron didn't want or need—he'd never know if his tirade at R.J. that morning had caused his brother to rush so much that he was careless and fell off the scaffolding. He'd probably always believe he was responsible. He carried enough guilt around, without adding his brother's death to the list. And Wyatt. Exhaling heavily, he looked to the endless blue sky above for an answer, a measure of peace from the terrible conflict that tore at him.

The trout rose, then darted away, like Cimarron, not yet brave enough to take the bait. Roll casting, Cimarron set the fly near the boulders again and again, searching for the elusive trout, but he found concentrating difficult today.

He hadn't fathered that child. Why in hell would R.J. saddle him with a lifelong responsibility? There had to be other avenues. Adoption. Foster care. Something. Anything!

Then he felt the satisfying jolt. His trout was back. The fly disappeared. Line taut, rod bent double, the reel squealed as the trout ran. Cimarron played him, let him run, patiently stripping the struggling fish in. Its scales glinted silver in the sunlight as it leaped for freedom.

Unpleasant memories disappeared from Cimarron's mind with the thrill of conquest. He could just stay right here in Little Lobo, guard his house from Sarah's wrecking ball and fish until his problems resolved themselves.

"You got one, Unca Cimron!" Wyatt pranced along the bank. "You got a big one!"

Jolted from his concentration, Cimarron flinched. The trout took advantage of the slack line and escaped. Even had the gall to give a victory leap a few yards away before vanishing. Cimarron swore the damn fish grinned at him.

"Why the hell did you do that?" Cimarron shouted, turning to the child. "You made me lose my fish. Can't you do anything..."

Wyatt crumbled visibly, his shoulders quivering as he backed away.

Right. Cimarron bit back the word. What was *he* doing? Saying the same devastating things to his young nephew that had so often sent him scurrying for a hiding place before his father could see the tears and give him still more grief. He was becoming the man his father had been.

"Hell, no!" he muttered. He sloshed to shore. "Look, Wyatt, I'm sorry I yelled."

But the damage was done. The child retreated to the spot where he'd sat to eat, hugged his knees and hid his face. Cimarron squatted in front of him.

"Wyatt, look at me."

Wyatt shook his head.

"I shouldn't have yelled at you, it's just that the fish got..."

Got away. So what? It was a damn fish. He would have released it anyway.

Cimarron reached out to touch Wyatt's shoulder but stopped short. He shook his head and stood up. What was the point? He didn't know how to get through to the kid. He was rotten at this daddy charade anyway. He had to find a good, loving home for his nephew—with two parents who knew what they were doing.

From the corner of his eye, Cimarron saw a flash of movement. Adrenaline jolted his system.

"Don't move, Wyatt," he commanded softly. The child reacted by lifting his head to look at Cimarron. "Don't move. Stay real still."

CHAPTER SIX

SARAH PRESSED HARD against the cordless screwdriver, forcing the screw into the brittle wood. The soft whirring sound grew weaker by the moment as her batteries lost power.

"Just two more," she begged between clenched teeth. She drove another one flush with the plate of the metal hasp. Her screwdriver finally ground to a stop with a few threads left on the last screw, but the result was good enough.

This was her third latch. She'd been lucky that Harry Upshaw was willing to bring them to her while she finished cleaning up in the café after breakfast. She didn't tell him why she wanted them and she wouldn't let him put them on for two reasons. One, it might actually be against the law to padlock the property if Cimarron's claim was legal, and she didn't want Harry to get in trouble; and two, she wanted the personal satisfaction of being the one to lock out the man who had stolen her property. Furthermore, she didn't want Harry or anybody else to know about her predicament right now. Replacing the screwdriver in her toolbox, she threaded a heavy padlock through the loop and snapped it closed, as she'd done on the other two doors of the old house.

"There, maybe that'll keep him out for now."

She peered across the valley, expecting to see Cimarron return from fishing any minute. She'd watched from her bedroom window early that morning as he stalked off down the trail, fishing gear in hand, with his cute little boy trotting hard to keep up. She wondered about the story behind their odd standoffish relationship but told herself she probably was better off not knowing.

Glad to finish her chore without being caught, she hurried back home and put away the tools, then changed into jeans, boots and a sweater and locked her own doors. She got into her small SUV and pulled onto the main road in the direction of the Rocking R Ranch. She needed to get away, to put distance between herself and her problem; to spend the day in the fresh air and solicit advice from Kaycee, who had been her best friend ever since she'd opened the clinic next door to the café two years ago. Sarah loved spending time at the ranch. Something fun was always happening on Sunday afternoons and the high spirits of the kids were contagious.

As usual, Sarah was greeted by two Australian shepherds and a mutt named Sam that Kaycee had rescued. Four of the seven Rider children raced from the house, waving and shouting when they saw her, and not breaking stride until they disappeared into the darkness of the barn.

Kaycee greeted Sarah from a paddock across the graveled parking area where she waited with two saddled horses.

"Come on, I've got the horses saddled. Let's go for a ride."

"Wonderful," Sarah said, climbing the paddock fence to mount her favorite mare and follow Kaycee through the gate.

Kaycee's tawny hair was pulled into a ponytail that was looped through the back of a baseball cap. Tall, slender and athletic, Kaycee could manhandle a yearling steer with the best of men and had earned the respect of even the surliest ranchers for her knowledge and quiet competence as a large-animal vet.

A woman vet in a tough, mostly male environment, Kaycee could hold her own. Yet Sarah had seen her in tears, too, torn between the career she'd worked hard to build and the man she loved. Sarah would bet Kaycee's vet skills weren't what ultimately won the heart of widowed rancher Jon Rider. Probably it had more to do with the smile that lit her green eyes and the loving, nurturing disposition that allowed her to become an instant mother to seven kids under the age of twelve. Never in her wildest dreams could Sarah imagine becoming an overnight mother and suddenly having seven kids. It boggled the mind. Sarah missed having Kaycee living next door at the clinic, but she would never begrudge her friend the happiness that was reflected in her face every day since she'd fallen in love.

Given a loose rein, the horses meandered along the mountain path. Sarah lifted her face to the warm sunshine, enjoying the peace, letting the gentle sway of the horse's back relax her a little.

Kaycee gave her time to wind down for a few minutes before she said, "You sounded upset when you called this morning. Everything okay?"

"No," Sarah said abruptly. "Oh, Kaycee, all my wonderful plans have fallen through. My bed-and-breakfast...Everything." Sarah pressed her lips together to keep from crying. That never solved anything and besides, Kaycee was so strong...She'd never let anybody steal her dreams and neither would Sarah.

"How?" Kaycee turned in the saddle and tilted her head toward Sarah. "What's going on?"

"Some guy just showed up out of the blue yesterday and claimed he owns my bed-and-breakfast. That Bobby sold it to him."

"No way! That can't be right. Bobby wouldn't do that, would he?"

"Yes," Sarah said with a huff. "Yes, he probably would, if it meant money."

"You saw where he signed it over?"

"No, I was too mad to look at anything, but Griff came by last night and checked him out because the nut decided to sleep in his pickup truck in my parking lot. Griff told me that the signature sure looked liked Bobby's. No criminal background. The sign on the side of his truck claims he's a restoration expert. Damn it, why did he choose my house to restore?"

"Did you ask him?"

"No, I didn't even want to talk to him."

"You'll have to. You do plan to talk to a lawyer, right?"

"Yes, I'll call Nolan in the morning, as soon as I can. I hope there's something he can do."

Kaycee reined her horse to a stop on a bluff overlooking the sweeping river valley that ran between two majestic mountain ranges. Myriad shades of green and blue swirled together with the brilliant flowers of summer. They formed a soothing tapestry that seemed to bring Sarah's problems into a more manageable focus. Surely she could work something out with this guy. Or break the contract. She was anxious now to talk to her lawyer, to see what options she might have.

Kaycee leaned on her saddle horn, gazing into the misty distance. "You said he has a sign on his truck. Does he have a Web site? Maybe you could learn more about him."

Sarah nodded. "Good idea. I've been so overwhelmed since yesterday, I haven't been able to put two thoughts together. First Aaron didn't show and my grill finally cratered. Then this guy comes in and drops a bombshell on me. He did fix my grill, though, and he helped me with dinner last night."

Kaycee looked askance at her. "Wait. He buys your house, and then you let him help you out?"

"I know, I know. Stupid. But honestly, I wouldn't have made it without help. Sometimes you do what you have to do, to just get by."

"Let's ride back and take a look at this guy, if we can find him on the Net."

When they had unsaddled the horses and put them out to pasture, Sarah and Kaycee closeted themselves in Kaycee's home office in the rear of the rambling ranch house. Kaycee made coffee in a pot on a side counter and they sat down to do a bit of research.

"What's the name of his company?"

Sarah repeated the company name she'd seen on the truck logo.

"His name is Cimarron Cole."

"Cimarron? Interesting name." Kaycee clicked the mouse a few times, searching. Within seconds, over a thousand hits popped up.

"Wow," Sarah said softly.

"Wow is right," Kaycee agreed. The first entry was his Web site. She clicked. "Double wow."

The impressive home page was a sophisticated layout with photos floating across the page, fading and merging. Always there was the same sequence. First, photos from several angles of a house in terrible shape, and then a montage of construction scenes, ending with spectacular restorations.

Kaycee slid the mouse to Sarah. "You go where you want to."

Sarah began clicking links to various projects Cimarron had done—the final results always breathtaking. She leaned forward in her chair, with a different perspective now. Okay, so he could do what he said. In fact, he could make her house more grand than she'd ever dreamed it could be. His house. Not hers. She felt the sting of tears again. She wanted her bed-and-breakfast so much it hurt. She'd anticipated the excitement of different guests each week. She just wanted things to be the way they were before.

She clicked on his bio, and a photo of him popped up, along with a statement of his professional creed. No hint of family or personal information.

"Is that him?" Kaycee said, eyebrows raised.

"It is."

"He's a hunk."

Sarah gave a wry grin. "He looks better in person. For what it's worth."

"Dang, Sarah. Too bad he's the villain."

"Yeah. Too bad. He's got a sweet little boy with him, too, about the twins' age."

"That's interesting. No wife?"

"Not that I know of. And he doesn't seem to want the child at all."

"Looks like you've got a plateful, all of a sudden."

"More than I ever wanted, I assure you."

Another click brought her to a page that listed the homes Cimarron had restored or refurbished. At the beginning of his career he'd apparently contracted out to others, restoring private family homes and historically relevant property.

Over the years, those jobs had given way to his own projects. Before-and-after photos of each house had a short caption underneath noting the beginning and ending dates of each project and usually included photos of the smiling new owners. A plantation house he'd just completed in Louisiana was on the market for several million dollars. No doubt he realized a significant profit on every house, otherwise why would he keep doing it? He'd recover his investment in Sarah's house ten times over—when he sold it. Sarah's optimism caved, leaving an empty spot that opened up like a sinkhole and swallowed her future.

Kaycee ran her finger lightly down the screen along the list of houses and prices. "He flips houses. Restores them and sells them off."

"Looks like," Sarah murmured. "What am I going to do?"

"If you need help buying it back or paying a lawyer, you know Jon and I will do as much as we can."

Sarah put her hand over Kaycee's on the desk. A true friend, who would no doubt dish out plenty of money for her. But this wasn't Kaycee's battle.

"Thanks. I know you would, but I don't think it would do any good. I can see why he's dead set on restoring the house and making a killing off it. But you never can tell...Maybe fate will intervene."

CHAPTER SEVEN

CIMARRON SLANTED HIS EYES in the direction of the movement. Dry leaves rustled. The bushes across the clearing moved. A bear? Mountain lion? He didn't have a weapon with him. Stupid mistake.

"Be still, Wyatt."

Barely breathing, he waited. There. He caught a glimpse of brown fur near the spot where he'd left the sandwiches. "Hey!"

"It's a dog," Wyatt cried, leaping to his feet.

Did nobody listen to him anymore? "Stay put," Cimarron snapped.

A big, hairy flop-eared dog looked up in surprise. Grabbing the jacket in its mouth, it bolted into the underbrush.

"Damn it! Come back here. That's my good jacket, you mutt."

So much for that. The dog was gone. Cimarron caught Wyatt by the shoulder of his jacket as the boy bounded off in pursuit.

"Don't run after that dog. We don't know anything about it. It might be sick or wild."

"Oh," Wyatt said in disappointment. "I wish it wasn't."

"Well, it probably is, so leave it alone. Time for us to get back anyway. And I told you to stay put. Why didn't you mind me?"

Wyatt lifted one shoulder and made a face. "Wanted to see the dog, I guess."

"Do what I tell you next time." Cimarron stared at the empty bush. "I liked that jacket."

Trying to shake off his frustration, he took his rod apart and gathered his gear, and they trekked back to civilization, looking around now and then at the sound of rustling leaves. Once he caught a glimpse of familiar brown fur and, still aggravated, he yelled at the dog to get lost. He lifted Wyatt to his shoulders. If the dog was feral, he might mistake Wyatt for prey.

The café parking lot was deserted, and Sarah's vehicle was gone from the carport behind the building. Just as well. He wanted to work in peace this afternoon. He had to make the house watertight before he could start any major repairs.

At the front door, however, Cimarron found a brand-new latch screwed into the original century-old wood and held fast with a padlock. So either Miss Sarah was handier with tools than she had let on or somebody like Deputy Dawg had come to her aid. Cursing softly, Cimarron traipsed around to the side and back doors, only to find both of them secured, as well. Frustrated, he yanked on the padlock on the back door.

"You can't get in, Unca Cimron?" Wyatt asked.

"Don't worry, I'll get in," Cimarron assured him. "I'll definitely get in."

He considered himself lucky she hadn't sent her personal deputy to tow his truck to the impound yard. Taking a screwdriver from a side toolbox, he unscrewed the hinged latch and removed it so she couldn't lock him inside later. Using the key Bobby had given him, he unlocked the back door and stepped through the doorway, momentarily satisfied with his small victory.

Light filtered in through tall, dirty kitchen windows that framed a striking view of the valley and mountains. Although the kitchen had been modernized in the fifties, the stove was old and nasty, certainly unusable, and the refrigerator was missing altogether. Cabinet doors hung open, some sprung and others attached by only one hinge. Cimarron moved on to the parlor.

Assessing the room for livability, Cimarron noted a fireplace in one corner, but he wouldn't risk lighting a fire until he had checked for breaches in the walls and chimney. A thick layer of gray dust covered every flat surface and cobwebs hung like lace from high corners. Debris littered the floor, and there were shards of glass from broken window-panes. Leaves, chunks of crumbling plaster and dirty reminders of the animals that had called this place home for a long time crunched underfoot. A couple of pieces of furniture had been pushed into one corner of the room away from the elements and were covered with limp, dingy sheets.

Wyatt peered around. "I don't like it in here."

"Might as well get used to it. We'll be staying here for a while."

"Do we have to? I like the truck better."

Cimarron looked down at him. "You planning to sleep out there by yourself? Because I'm staying in here."

Wyatt's lower lip extended in a pout, and he gave his surroundings another hard glare. "I guess it'll be okay in here," he said softly.

The kid wouldn't understand Cimarron's game plan to stake out his territory immediately and hopefully discourage Sarah's attempts to delay his progress. And if Cimarron told Wyatt he wouldn't be staying long, the child would want to know where they were going next and Cimarron wasn't up to breaking the news that only Wyatt would be moving on. He'd save that chore for a better day—if ever a better day came.

"It won't be so bad if we clean up some."

Cimarron made another trip to his truck and brought back a collapsible shovel, a well-worn push broom, leather work gloves and a roll of heavy-duty yard bags.

"You sweep all the trash in a pile with this broom and I'll pick it up and take it outside. Here, put these gloves on so you don't get splinters and get started. I'll be right back."

Cimarron took the time to remove the other two latches. He stashed the latches and padlocks in his truck to prevent Sarah from reusing them, Cimarron went back to the cleanup. He stopped in the doorway to watch Wyatt sweep. The man-size gloves reached almost to his elbows and he struggled to wrap his hands around the broom handle, long empty fingers splaying in all directions. But determination knit his brows together and he made choppy swipes at the dirty floor.

The kid took his business seriously, no doubt about that, even though he made little progress. Cimarron smiled at his nephew's diligent efforts, but the fleeting sense of attachment only made their precarious position more painful. He couldn't get attached to Wyatt—nor let Wyatt get comfortable with him. The inevitable parting would only be that much harder.

"How are you doing, buddy?" he said, shaking off the unwanted emotion.

"Good," Wyatt said, pointing to a clean spot that measured maybe a foot square.

"Keep it up, then. Clean off a place big enough for our sleeping bags." Cimarron took the shovel and began to scrape glass and debris into another pile, which he loaded into trash bags and carried outside.

After a while, Wyatt said, "I'm hungry."

"Me, too," Cimarron admitted, glancing in the general direction of the closed café. He hadn't eaten since the dog stole his breakfast. "We'll find something to eat when we're done here."

A few trash bags later, Cimarron surveyed the room. At least it was clear of rubbish and Wyatt had a slightly bigger spot cleaned on the wooden floor.

"How about switching jobs?" he said to the boy. "Sometimes if you do the same thing too long, you get sore."

Cimarron stretched his shoulders and Wyatt did the same.

"Okay." He handed over the broom.

"I'm going to get these cobwebs down. They're too high for you to reach anyway." Some were too high for Cimarron, too, but he brushed down quite a few of them.

"Are there spiders in there?" Wyatt asked, surveying Cimarron's progress closely.

"Nope. If they've got dust in them like these do, the spiders have moved away and left them long ago."

"I had a spider one time." Wyatt scraped at the cobwebs that drifted to the floor with the heavy shovel.

"You did? Where'd you get it?"

"It lived under the window in my room at one of our houses. Only came out at night when the lights were out."

"Then how did you know it was there?"

"Dead bug parts on the floor. Daddy said that the spider ate them at night. I saw him once when I got up to go to the bathroom."

"Guess you weren't scared, then."

"A little, but my daddy said the spider's mouth was too small to eat me, so I'd be okay."

Good ole R.J. Same thing he told me when I was a kid.

"Makes sense. You hold that shovel and I'm going to sweep the dirt on it so we can finish up here."

Wyatt concentrated on his new job, holding the shovel tight while Cimarron pushed the piles of dirt onto it and together they emptied the debris into a bag. Cimarron whistled softly and made wider sweeps to clean more of the floor than Wyatt had, without making a big deal of it. When he was satisfied, he tied the bag and he and Wyatt carried it out to join the others.

Late-afternoon shadows reached across the valley. Time had gotten away from him, and by now this small town had probably shut down for the day. He hadn't seen any restaurants on the way to Bozeman and, besides, everything might be closed on Sunday.

"Good thing we're guys," Cimarron said as he considered their options for cleaning up, since his newly purchased house didn't have running water.

"Why?"

Wyatt looked up at him with wide, inquisitive brown eyes. R.J.'s eyes. Damn, every time he looked at this kid, guilt as sharp and cutting as a buzz saw sliced through his middle. He couldn't offer Wyatt the life he deserved, yet he knew R.J.'s ghost would skewer him for giving the child away.

Cimarron made a show of sniffing under his arms. "Because we're both going to stink tonight. Nowhere to grab a shower."

"Oh, that. I don't care."

"Yeah, I know. Baths aren't your favorite thing." Cimarron glanced toward the closed café and the dark rooms above. "Then there's the problem of food."

Too bad the café wasn't open. Wonder where Sarah might be this afternoon? He was sure he'd hear from her once she discovered all her padlocks had been removed, but with his stomach growling he'd be glad to pay her for some leftovers.

"I like food," Wyatt said.

"Yep, but there's none to be had here. Let's ride around and see what we find."

They hopped into the truck. Wyatt stared out the side window at the passing scenery. He liked Montana better than anyplace he'd lived, but he missed his daddy. He couldn't figure out why he never came back to get him from his uncle's office that day. Wyatt overhead somebody say his daddy fell and got a "fatal," whatever that meant. When he asked his uncle Cimarron where his daddy was, Uncle Cimarron said he was probably in heaven. But Wyatt didn't know where that was, so he just had to wait until his daddy came to get him. But just in case he never did, which Wyatt was suspecting more and more, he didn't want to make his uncle Cimarron mad with him. Because if his uncle left him behind, he wouldn't have anywhere to go, and that scared Wyatt bad.

After a full tour of Little Lobo, which took all of half an hour, they were back where they started. Not a single quick mart or fast-food joint open.

"No food," Wyatt said in disappointment. "And my tummy's rumbling, too."

"We've got beans and franks in the back."

Wyatt screwed up his face.

"I'm not too happy about beans, either, considering the aftereffects," Cimarron said. "But at the moment I can't come up with any better option."

"Then we'll stink even more," Wyatt offered.

Cimarron laughed. "I guess we will. It's the price you pay for not having enough food. At least we won't be stuck in the truck."

Wyatt shrugged. "Guess so."

He helped his uncle bring in the ice chest that held their drinks, their sleeping bags, which they laid out in the parlor, and the small Porta Potti from the camper. Cimarron tacked a heavy canvas over the broken windows to keep out the draft, and then they sat on the front steps and spooned cold beans and franks from cans and watched the last rays of the sun fade to a golden sheen above the mountains.

"Pretty colors, huh?" Cimarron said.

Wyatt watched the sunset gradually fade, memorizing the shades so he could color a sunset later. "I like to color," he told his uncle.

"Yeah?"

"But I don't have a coloring book anymore." Or colors, Wyatt thought ruefully, just a bunch of broken crayons in the bottom of his backpack.

"We forgot to get it?"

"No, I colored it all up."

"Maybe one day we'll get to town and buy another one."

"Okay." Wyatt didn't want to push, but he hoped they made that trip soon. He just about went crazy worrying over stuff when he didn't have anything to do, but when he colored in his coloring books, he didn't think so much. He looked into his empty can. "My beans are all gone."

"Mine, too." Cimarron set the cans to one side and leaned back on his elbows, looking at the café. "I wonder where Sarah might be. I'm looking forward to a hot meal."

"Me, too." Wyatt leaned back like his uncle. "Tell me a story, Unca Cimron."

"I've told you every story I know."

"My daddy knew a lot of stories."

"Well, he had longer to learn stories than I've had. I don't know much about this daddy business."

"That's okay." And it was. Being his uncle was good enough right now. Just so he didn't go anywhere.

"Not really," Cimarron muttered, then louder, "You tired? Ready for bed?"

"Are you coming, too?" The last thing Wyatt wanted was to be alone in that dark, spooky house. If his uncle wasn't turning in, neither was he.

"I've got some work to do."

"Can I play in the camper till you go to bed?"

"Yeah, I guess so."

After he'd put Wyatt in the camper and opened the window between the cab and the camper shell, Cimarron sat down on the driver's side of the truck. Cimarron had a nice, if compact, office setup in the front seat of the truck, complete with a laptop and printer. Wyatt always rode in the backseat of the extended cab, so there'd been no need to rearrange or remove any of the equipment. He fired up his laptop, opening an architectural-design program. Keying in the approximate dimensions of the house, he started working on his restoration plans. Within a couple of hours, he had a good idea of what the building needed to survive and he knew without a doubt he would have a beauty when he was finished.

Sarah came home around eleven. She stopped outside her door to stare at the house, but she didn't venture up the hill. Too bad for Cimarron. He'd have begged some food from her. He watched as she went into the building, then followed the progression of lights-on-lights-off through the café and upstairs to her apartment. After a few minutes, her windows went dark and he wondered idly if she might be wide-awake like he was, worried and unsettled. He hadn't intended to throw her world into a state of upheaval, but he couldn't afford to lose the money he'd sunk in the house, especially since the Louisiana deal hadn't closed yet.

Besides, he thought, squirming in his seat to get more comfortable, he had no reason to feel guilty for making a good business deal. Anyway, she had ticked him off by padlocking the house. All inclination to go easy on her had dissipated during the half hour he'd spent removing the latches. Staring at the lighted computer screen filled with architectural renderings and notes, he heaved a sigh. All he had to do was get the place salable and he could put Sarah's pretty face and her problems behind him. She could deal with the new owners. Still didn't feel quite right, though, squashing her plans like that.

Cimarron yawned and shut down the laptop. In the camper, Wyatt was curled up asleep in the midst of his toys. Cimarron carefully pulled him out, set the alarm on the truck and headed off to bed in the cavernous old house.

• • • •

TURNING OVER in his sleeping bag a few hours later, Cimarron encountered a lump that hadn't been there when he went to sleep. Forcing his eyes open, he noticed slivers of sunlight squeezing around the canvas nailed over the windows. He moved his hand along the outside of his sleeping bag until he encountered the lump. Wyatt, still snug in his sleeping bag, had scooted across the floor and was butted up against Cimarron's back, making a warm spot through the thick material. Cimarron lay still a few minutes more, until thoughts of a hot breakfast at the café stirred him to action.

He eased from the sleeping bag, stood and flexed the kinks out of his shoulders. Disappointment waited at the door. Looking out, he saw no signs of activity at the café, even though it was well past opening

time. Then he saw Sarah sitting at a patio table, sipping coffee and reading a newspaper.

A broad deck, with several seating areas and a large covered grill,
ran the length of the building from Sarah's carport past the back door
of the café to another wider porch on the opposite end. There a door
protected by a storm screen and centered between curtained windows
on either side indicated the possibility of a room or apartment. The
building itself was turn-of-the-century, constructed of regional stone
and white clapboard siding. As he watched, Sarah poured another cup
of coffee, showing no indication of going to work anytime soon.

The woman ran a café, for Pete's sake. Why wasn't it open? He was
hungry and Wyatt would be starving.

So on to plan B. Get the kid up and go in search of food. The hour-
long round-trip drive to Livingston hadn't been penciled in on his
agenda this morning and the inconvenience threatened to put him in a
bad mood at the start of the day.

He considered the best time to have a chat with Sarah about the
padlocks—before finding food or after. Probably after would be better,
when stomachs were full. He would be a bit more mellow and Wyatt
would be willing to play a while by himself. He turned away from the
window to the sleeping child.

"Wyatt," he called, gently shaking Wyatt's shoulders. "Let's get going."

"Where?" Wyatt asked in a drowsy voice.

"We've got to find some breakfast. The café's not open."

Wyatt sat up, scratching his stomach and yawning. "Aww...I'm really hungry."

"Me, too, so let's get moving."

They left by the front door, Cimarron locking it behind them.
Sarah looked up, saw them on the front porch, and, even from a distance, Cimarron could see a scowl darken her face.

"Uh-oh, we're in for trouble."

"Why?" Wyatt said, following Cimarron's gaze. "She's mad?"

"Looks like. Let's go." He bundled Wyatt into the backseat and trotted around the truck, stepping up into the driver's seat.

"You scared of her, Unca Cimron?"

Cimarron glanced in the rearview mirror at him. "Scared? Me? No. But do you want to waste half the morning arguing with her? I thought you were hungry."

"I am."

"All right, then."

Cimarron started the engine, but before he could shift into Drive, Sarah was beside the truck with her hand on his door handle. Jerk her arm off or lower the window and talk to her—why did he have to think about that for a second?

From the backseat he heard Wyatt's quiet "Uh-oh."

Through the window, Sarah's eyes shot fire. *Uh-oh.*

Powering down the window, Cimarron gave her a wide grin. "Good morning."

"How did you get into my house?" She laid long, smooth fingers on the window frame, as if holding him there.

"My house," Cimarron corrected, still smiling. "Oddly enough, somebody had trespassed on my property and put padlocks on all the doors. I believe there might be a lawsuit in that."

She glared at him. "I doubt it. Until I'm sure those documents of yours are legal, I consider that my house. Dare I hope you're leaving for good?"

"Nope. Just going for food. I've got a kid back there starving half to death because this town pulls in the sidewalks on Sunday."

"Maybe you need to move on then, because that's what we do."

"Oh, I'll be moving on in time."

"Sure. After you flip my house to more strangers or some corporation."

"Been checking up on me, have you?" Something about that pleased Cimarron, although he couldn't exactly say why. Well, maybe he did know why. A hot babe like Sarah checking him out—worked every time. But she didn't need to know that.

"Yes, and I wasn't impressed," she said.

"Well, I'll have to see what I can do about that."

She frowned and her mouth drew into a very kissable pout; however, he knew better than to try that if he wanted to keep his own lips attached to his face. "I don't think so, Mr. Cole."

"Cimarron. Might as well be on a first-name basis since—"

"I'm really hungry," Wyatt whined. "Can we go now?"

"In a minute." Cimarron turned his attention back to Sarah. "Anyway, I hope you're going to take care of the legal inquiries today. I need to start working."

She narrowed her eyes at him like a cat considering whether to keep torturing her prey or go in for the kill. "I don't know if I'll have time. I have to get in touch with my lawyer and he's very busy, too."

"I see. Well, here's the bottom line. The sale was legal." He shuffled a few papers around on the seat beside him until he found a manila folder. Taking out a thick envelope, he handed it to her. "Here's a copy of the sales contract. Let your lawyer validate it. Because I'm going to restore this house. And I'm going to start this week. Whether you get your legal questions answered or not."

"Oh, really?"

Cimarron put the truck in gear and cocked an eyebrow at her. "Really."

She jerked her hand away from the window and stepped back, an angry frown on her face.

Cimarron hesitated.

"Let's go! I want something to eat real bad," Wyatt said.

Sarah turned her back on him and strode down the hill.

"Yeah. Me, too," Cimarron muttered as he drove past Sarah before she reached the café, then turned onto the highway toward town.

CHAPTER EIGHT

SARAH WANTED to cry. Alone in the café, she went from table to table filling the salt and pepper shakers and wondering how her life had taken such a nosedive in a couple of days all because of Bobby's selfishness. Bobby had no right...no right at all!

She sat down at a table and stared out the window. The café was closed on Mondays, so she wouldn't have to put up a good front today. And Cimarron Cole was gone for the moment. He hadn't taken long to dismantle her padlocks and get back into the house. Why did he have to latch on to her property, anyway? Why not any other ramshackle house in Montana except hers?

"Oohhh," she muttered, shoving the shakers back in place in the middle of the table. She rubbed her palms across her cheeks, scrubbing away tears that had leaked out in spite of her best efforts to stanch them. The envelope of papers lay on the table beside her and she took them out and spread them across the table. The last sheet was covered with signatures. Cimarron Cole's bold, sure stroke, the scribble of a lawyer, the dainty writing of a notary and her brother's inimitable scrawl.

She read over the document from beginning to end, her heart sinking with every paragraph, then sucked in a surprised breath when she saw what Cimarron had paid her brother. Her paltry offer paled in comparison. No wonder Bobby had sold out on her. But that didn't make her less outraged. They'd had a deal and they were family.

She pulled the cell phone from the clip on her belt and dialed her brother's number. He hadn't answered her calls so far, but she was going to keep pestering him until he did.

To her surprise, this time Bobby answered—after she'd let it ring forever.

"I can't believe you picked up," she said. "I've been calling you non-stop for two days."

"Figured I couldn't avoid you the rest of my life. Sorry about the house."

"Why did you do this to me?" She fought to keep the quaver out of her voice. "We had a deal. That's family property."

"I didn't have any choice. I was in a bind."

"In a bind? A bind, Bobby? You sold Uncle Eual's house because you were in a bind? I can't believe you're saying that."

"Stop shouting at me, sis. I swear I didn't have a choice. I got in a lot of trouble gambling, and some guys were threatening my kneecaps if I didn't pay off soon. I knew Cole wanted the house and had the money. Which you didn't."

Fury made Sarah's hand shake and she pressed the phone hard against her ear. "We had a commitment, Bobby. We were supposed to keep our properties together. Uncle Eual wanted that, and you know it."

"But he didn't put it in the will, and I needed the money."

"Did you even pay off your debts, or can I expect the goons to show up here?"

"I paid it."

"Then blew the rest on an RV and a floozie."

"Look, don't talk about Sunni like that. She's a nice girl and we got married."

"So I heard. Where are you now?"

"In Fort Lauderdale."

"Wonderful. You and Sunni in sunny Florida. I hope she gets a great tan."

"Oh, believe me, she will."

She wished she could reach through the phone and wipe off that smile she heard in his voice. He never took anything seriously, and this marriage probably wouldn't fare any better than his first two had.

"You could have at least told me. This guy just showed up here."

He came back with his usual immature logic. "I knew, if I told you, you'd have a fit and try to stop me. I hated to do it, but you can't imagine how bad I needed that money. Look on the bright side, sis, he's a good-looking rich guy. He's, like, a world-famous restoration expert. He can fix up that bed-and-breakfast like you and me never could. And if you play your cards right, you could get it back for next to nothing."

"What do you mean by that?"

"La-di-da. You know what I mean. You scratch his back, or whatever, and he'll build your house. Besides, you need a husband. You'll end up an old maid at the rate you're going. I'm doing you a favor."

He sounded serious!

Sarah was dumbstruck. At least Bobby must have taken her sputtering for what it was—a fuse burning real short on a load of dynamite. He hung up before she exploded.

Almost immediately the phone rang again. Thinking it must be Bobby calling back, she answered without checking caller ID.

"What?" she said sharply.

"Sarah? This is Nolan Birchfield returning your call. How are you?"

"Nolan? I'm so sorry. I thought you were my brother. Thanks for calling back. I've got a problem."

Sarah explained her predicament to her lawyer, whose office she'd called first thing that morning. He'd been in court, but the receptionist promised to give him Sarah's message the minute he came in. Nolan set up an appointment with her for an hour later in his offices in Livingston. She just had time to get dress and get there, so she changed clothes and hit the road immediately.

"So you're having more trouble with your brother?" Nolan said, showing her to a chair when she arrived.

Sitting in Nolan's wood-paneled office, Sarah felt the last of her hope dissipate, along with her dreams, as Nolan, impeccably dressed and exuding legal wisdom, explained in his confident soft-spoken voice that while she might have had a verbal agreement with Bobby, it would be hard to enforce, since Cimarron seemed to have an airtight contract. He cautioned Sarah that a legal battle would be costly, maybe driving her into debt that she couldn't afford and threatening the café.

The idea of losing her café on top of the rest was the final straw. After leaving Nolan's office, she slumped into the driver's seat of her car and considered having a major pity party. But every time she thought of what Bobby had done to her, the urge to scream overrode the temptation to cry.

Enough of that! Let two stupid guys kill my dreams? Not a chance. Get a plan.

She lifted her head from her arms, which were crossed on the steering wheel, squared her shoulders and sniffed. All right, so she couldn't break the contract and she didn't know how she could afford to buy back her house right now, but that didn't mean she had to make things easy for Cimarron Cole or let Bobby off the hook. Her padlocks hadn't been much of a deterrent, so maybe she needed to try another tack, some other way to discourage him and make him wish he'd never seen Little Lobo.

Too bad Bobby was right. Kaycee had pointed it out, too. Cimarron was a hunk, and under other circumstances...

Forget it, Sarah. Don't be an idiot. He's the enemy.

If she could just delay his progress on the house long enough, surely she could find a way to raise the money to buy him out. On the drive home, she tried to think of anybody and everybody who might loan her money or become an investor in her bed-and-breakfast. The first thing she needed was a firm price from Cimarron before he started working on the house—as low as he would go.

By the time she arrived home, she'd lost half a day that she should have spent doing prep for the café tomorrow. She got busy immediately, taking out her ire on the vegetables on her cutting board, envisioning the heads of the two men responsible for messing up her life there on the chopping block. Just as the tedium of soothing and familiar habit began to calm her somewhat, she heard Cimarron's pickup truck crunch across the parking lot and move up the hill behind the house.

Let the games begin!

• • • •

CIMARRON MADE NOTE of Sarah's vehicle in the carport and saw that the back door of the café was open. Good, he needed to talk to her. But first, the truck had to be unloaded.

"Here, Wyatt, you take this bag." He handed Wyatt a plastic bag containing coloring books, picture and storybooks, crayons and a couple of toys. If he managed to start on the house soon, he would need to keep Wyatt busy and out of the way.

After a few trips, all their purchases were transferred to the house. No more beans for a while, hopefully. Cimarron had bought a two-burner camp stove and a small refrigerator, along with a couple of folding chairs and two camp cots, so they wouldn't have to sleep on the floor. Groceries included bread, fruit and juice boxes for Wyatt. Cimarron routinely kept a small pot, frying pan and utensils in the truck. They had stopped at a fast-food place in Livingston and filled their grumbling stomachs and they'd also brought home some fried chicken for Wyatt to snack on later. Last, Cimarron brought in the ice chest from the back of the truck, filled with sandwich meat, eggs, cheese and milk.

"I'm going to talk to the lady at the café. I'll be right back."

"No, I want to come. I don't want to stay here."

Cimarron swallowed his impatience. "Come then. But you're going to have to get over this being-my-shadow thing. I want to start working next week, and then you'll have to play by yourself."

Wyatt's eyes glittered with tears and he blinked hard. "I don't like it here."

"Well, get used to it. No other choice for now. Dry up and let's go."

Sarah worked at the prep table, her back to the screen door. She wore a long white apron over her clothes and had clipped her hair at the back of her neck with a big barrette.

"Take that!" she told a bell pepper as she sliced off the top and gutted it. "And you, take this." The onion she split in half rocked uncertainly on the counter.

"I hope that's not intended to be me." Cimarron's voice startled her, but she turned and looked at him boldly.

"No, you were the bell pepper. I ripped your insides out."

"Ouch. You're hell with that knife."

"Long years of practice."

Cimarron gave her a wry smile. "I guess you heard from Bobby or your lawyer, then."

"Both. I hate being wrong," she muttered, turning back to her work, madly dicing the onion, sending little chunks flying all over the counter.

"I tried to tell you the contract couldn't be broken."

"I know. And about Bobby, too."

She kept working and Cimarron hung back, eyeing the monstrous blade in her hand, which she wielded like a samurai.

"Look," he said after a few moments of silence. "I know you're upset..."

"How much will it take to buy my house back from you—as it stands."

"Around a million and a half."

Sarah laid the knife down, her hands trembling. "You've got to be kidding. You didn't pay Bobby that much for it."

"True. But I paid Bobby what he asked for it, not what it's worth. I try not to lose money on a deal."

"I'll pay you what you paid Bobby. That's only fair."

"It's not business, though. I have to make some money off this house. I've turned down other offers and missed a chance at another good project because I'm here. I can't just break even."

"How long can you give me?"

"A week. I'm lining up my contractors this week, so I can start work next Monday."

"A week? That's not fair. You probably couldn't come up with that much money in a week."

Cimarron heard the despair in her voice and had some qualms. If only he'd known she wanted the place before he made the deal with Bobby...

"Do you think you can raise that kind of money? Realistically?"

"Yes," she said stubbornly, without turning around. "I'm not destitute, you know. But not in a week."

"I didn't say you were." Cimarron fidgeted, not wanting his tone of voice to betray the doubt he felt. "A month? That's all the time I can afford to lose. So, you'll let me know as soon as you can?"

"Yes."

"Then, let me ask a favor. I need to hook up to your electricity for a couple of days until I get somebody out here to check the wiring and get it turned on."

"I don't think so."

Cimarron moved to the prep table so he could see Sarah's face. "Why?"

She shrugged, ducking her head over her work. "I don't want you living up there and I can't afford to waste electricity if I'm going to have to buy the place back."

"We're already living there. It would just be nice to have a little light and a working refrigerator."

"Go to the motel down the road."

"In the first place, I don't want to stay there. I like to be close to my work."

"You're not going to be doing any work."

"We'll see. And second, the motel is full. I stopped by on the way to Livingston, trying to get a room long enough to shower and shave, but I couldn't. So that's out. Sarah?" Cimarron leaned down, cocked his head and stared at her until she glanced at him with eyes cold enough to freeze him where he stood. "At least you could cooperate a little. I did agree to give you an opportunity to buy the place back."

She turned those icy eyes full on him. "Right. A month. Big favor."

"Better than nothing," Cimarron said, piqued by her attitude. "Forget the electric hookup. We'll be fine until I get the power company out here. I filled out the forms today for an independent hookup. I had a feeling I might run into this sort of sh—Stuff."

"Just go away."

"Gone. Come on, Wyatt."

"Are we going to have to stay in that scary old house in the dark again?" Wyatt asked as Cimarron caught his hand and led him out of the café. "I don't *like* it in there in the dark!"

"It'll be okay. You gotta get past being scared of the dark."

"How?"

"I don't know right off, but anyway I bought a battery-operated lantern today. We'll have a little light."

At the house, Cimarron settled Wyatt down in the parlor with a coloring book and crayons to keep him busy. For the rest of the afternoon, Cimarron worked to clear more of the accumulation of debris from the downstairs area. He found the water valve and turned it on, then did a quick but thorough inspection of the interior, looking for any leaks that might spell disaster. Satisfied, he tried the faucet in the kitchen. With a great show of rattling, gurgling and spitting, it produced some nasty water. As soon as he was sure the drain worked, he set the water to a steady flow and went on to the downstairs bathroom. He took the lid off the toilet, checked the inside and found the float rotted. But he'd anticipated that and had a spare in the truck.

The seal around the bottom looked okay, so as soon as he changed the float, he turned the water on to the toilet, closed his eyes, said a quick prayer and flushed. More nasty water, but the toilet worked and after a few flushes the water looked better. It would suffice for now.

With supplies that he'd bought in Livingston, he cleaned both the kitchen and bathroom. He hadn't really planned to do the domestic routine again after his mother died, and yet he'd cooked and cleaned more in the two days he'd been in Little Lobo than in all the past twelve years combined.

All the while, he stewed about Sarah. Everything had gone south on him about the time he bought this house, and he was beginning to believe it might turn into his personal albatross. His plans for life had barreled onto a side road to nowhere, and he had no idea how to put on the brakes. Not in his wildest imagination did he believe Sarah could come up with the money to buy back her house in a month or a lifetime. She'd risk everything she had, including the café, and never be able to turn the house into a bed-and-breakfast.

Maybe when he got the situation with Wyatt worked out, he'd see more options, but for now he needed to settle down and regroup. And he had to get his money out of the house. He could cut Sarah only so much of a deal, no matter how much he empathized with her problem—or how sexy she looked when she was mad.

"Unca Cimron, I can't see to color anymore. How about turning on that light?"

"How about we get cleaned up and make a sandwich."

"Okay," Wyatt said, the disappointment clear in his voice.

Cimarron put away the cleaning materials, washed his hands well and ran a hand through his hair. They both needed baths badly, but a sponge bath would be the extent of their cleanup for tonight.

"Then we'll take a look at those storybooks."

After a chilly wash for both of them, Cimarron put Wyatt into flannel pajamas and warm socks. He changed into clean jeans, a sweatshirt and loafers. They ate sandwiches and drinks from the ice chest. He'd been looking forward to a nice hot dinner until he noticed the business hours of the Little Lobo Eatery and Daily Grind. No lunch or dinner on Sunday and no food at all on Monday. Now he didn't know if he wanted to darken Sarah's door for breakfast, either, considering her attitude. Except that Wyatt had to eat, and Cimarron's fare of late probably wasn't the best for a growing child. Another reason he didn't need a kid.

He switched on the camping lantern and took it and a book over to the cots in the center of the room. Wyatt snuggled up beside him and watched as Cimarron turned to the table of contents and read the titles of the different stories.

"Which one do you want to hear?" Cimarron asked.

"Can I see the pictures?"

"Does that help you decide?"

"Yes."

Cimarron gave the book to Wyatt so he could turn the pages and find a story.

"This one," Wyatt pointed to *The Cat in the Hat*.

"Okay. What's the name of it?"

Wyatt puzzled over the words for a moment. "Don't know."

Cimarron put his finger under the word *cat*. "Do you know that word?"

Again Wyatt shook his head. Cimarron moved his finger to the word *the*.

"That one?"

"No."

"Do you know any words?"

"I don't think so."

"The alphabet?"

Wyatt looked at him with puzzled eyes.

"The ABCs?"

This time the child gave no response.

"Can you count?"

"One two three four five six seven eight nine ten."

"That's it? As far as you can go?"

"Yes." Wyatt's voice quavered the least bit. "Am I supposed to know more?"

Cimarron looked down at the book. He strongly suspected a five-year-old should know much more, but Wyatt looked stricken, so Cimarron just shrugged and said, "I don't know. Probably not. We'll worry about that later. For now, let's read *The Cat in the Hat*."

Cimarron put his finger under each word as he read it, and Wyatt paid rapt attention. At the end of the story, Wyatt put his finger on the page and said proudly, "That word's *cat*."

"Hey, you're right. Quick learner."

"And that word's *hat*."

"Right again. Pretty soon, you'll be reading to me. Now, you get into bed. We're going to do a lot of work in this old house tomorrow."

"You going to bed, too?" Wyatt asked as he wiggled into his sleeping bag.

"In a few minutes." Cimarron zipped the bag halfway up. "Don't roll off that bed tonight."

"You going to stay in here?"

"Yes, Wyatt, I'll be here. Now close your eyes and go to sleep. I've got some work to do on the computer."

Soon Wyatt's soft breathing and the clicking of the laptop keyboard were the only sounds in the still house, and when Cimarron's cell phone chimed, the sound echoed loudly off the walls. He answered before it rang a second time.

"Hold on a second," he said, quickly setting down the laptop on the cot and going outside to the porch. A bright moon hung over the distant mountains and the night had grown cold. "Sorry, I couldn't talk inside."

"Cimarron? This is Walt." Walt Ambrose was a family-practice at-torney in partnership with the corporate attorneys Cimarron used for business transactions.

The few weeks he'd had Wyatt had confirmed what Cimarron sus-pected: he was not father material. Wyatt deserved a stable home with two parents, not the vagabond lifestyle that Cimarron loved. So he had checked out a few adoption agencies and Social Services, then decided to look into private adoption. One way seemed like sending the child into the great unknown and the other reeked of selling him, but he had to do something before they became attached to one another—some-thing Cimarron fought harder every day that passed.

"Yes, thanks for calling back, Walt."

During their first discussion, the lawyer had asked a slew of difficult questions about Wyatt's situation and Cimarron's authority to adopt the child out.

"I've put out feelers in several directions. As I told you before, it's far harder to place a five-year-old. Most couples want a newborn."

"I appreciate your help."

"I wanted to keep you updated, and I also thought we should dis-cuss the pros and cons of the open adoption you mentioned."

"I'd like the option of being able to keep in touch with him, since I'm the only family he has left."

Walt described several situations where open adoption might cause problems for those involved, especially when it became confusing for the child. Still, Cimarron thought he wanted to go that way, out of re-spect for R.J.

"How long do you anticipate this taking?" Cimarron asked.

"Weeks, maybe months."

"I see," Cimarron said, the tension in his midsection becoming al-most unbearable.

"You should realize I might not be able to find a suitable adoptive family at all."

"I know. I'll deal with that if I have to."

"Fine, I'll be in touch."

Cimarron stuck the cell phone in his pocket and sat wearily on the steps, crossing his arms across his chest and hunkering down against the rising wind. What if he couldn't find a good home for Wyatt? All he wanted for his nephew was a decent life—something he'd never had with his own dysfunctional family. Why did it have to be so damn heartbreaking?

Listening to the peaceful night sounds, Cimarron laid his head on his arms. He must have dozed, but then he jerked up, fully awake, momentarily confused by his surroundings. A piercing shriek from inside the house brought him to his feet. He rushed in, thinking Wyatt was hurt.

The child was sitting up on his cot screaming hysterically. Cimarron held him, trying to figure out what was wrong. Wyatt clamped his arms around Cimarron's neck, sobbing.

"I want my daddy! I don't like it in here! I want my daddy!"

"It's okay. It's okay, Wyatt. I'm right here."

"I don't like it here. You said you wasn't going anywhere! I want my daddy!"

Cimarron patted Wyatt's back, trying to comfort him. The child only howled louder.

"Come on, Wyatt. It's okay. We'll go outside, all right? There's a big moon. Stop crying now."

Wyatt kicked and squirmed, trying to get loose, but Cimarron wasn't sure if the child was awake or having a nightmare, so he held on to him, walking from one end of the long front porch to the other, wheedling, begging, bribing the child to hush, to no avail.

Good thing there weren't close neighbors. They'd think he was trying to kill the kid.

CHAPTER NINE

"**WHAT'S HE DOING?** Killing the kid?" Sarah muttered.

She sat up in bed, listening to the wails coming from the old house through her open window. She rose and pulled on jeans and a sweatshirt over her pajamas, then slipped her feet into moccasins and found a flashlight. Child abuse was one thing she would not tolerate.

The screaming intensified as Sarah climbed the slope to the house. A dim lantern sat on the top step and Cimarron was pacing the porch with the struggling child in his arms. Sarah stopped at the bottom of the steps.

"What's wrong?" she called.

Cimarron stopped, a wave of relief washing over his face.

"Is he hurt?" she said.

His face, in the glow of the lantern, looked pale and haunted. "I don't know. I don't know what to do with him."

"What do you mean?"

"Just what I said. I don't know what to do. I don't think he's hurt. I think he had a nightmare, but I can't get him to be still long enough to be sure."

Sarah climbed the steps and laid her hand on Wyatt's damp forehead. He jerked away. "He's hot, but that's probably from crying and not fever. Wyatt?" she said quietly. "Wyatt, will you come to me for a few minutes?" Gently but firmly, she loosened his death grip on Cimarron's neck and took him, still fighting, into her arms.

She rubbed the sweaty child's back. "Get a blanket for him. He's going to catch a cold out here, damp like this."

"I don't have a blanket. We sleep in sleeping bags."

Sarah frowned. This man was rich as hell, according to his Web site, yet he was living like a hobo.

"Come on." She led the way down the hill to the café, where she directed Cimarron to a key hanging behind the door. "That's to the efficiency next door."

Cimarron unlocked the apartment and stood aside so that Sarah could go in first with Wyatt.

"There are blankets in there." Sarah pointed to a closet. Wyatt wept noisily on her shoulder.

Sarah held his head against her shoulder and helped Cimarron wrap a blanket around him.

"I want my daddy," Wyatt sobbed, his voice hoarse from crying. "I want to go home."

"Your daddy's right here. He's not going anywhere."

Wyatt slung his head violently back and forth. "I want my daddy."

Sarah gave Cimarron a long, hard look. The resemblance between them was remarkable, but she needed to be sure. "You are his father, aren't you?"

"I'm his uncle. His father's dead. A month ago. This is the first time he's acted like this."

Sarah hugged the child closer, uneasy with the situation. This man had shown up out of nowhere with the deed to her house and a child she'd assumed was his son. Now she had to wonder, was this child safe—and was she? What had happened to his father, his mother? Sarah intended to get some answers, but first she needed to calm the boy enough to be sure he wasn't injured in some way.

She began to hum a lullaby, rubbing slow circles on his back as she gently rocked him back and forth. The squalling slowed to intermittent sobs, then snuffling. Finally Wyatt laid his head against her neck and fell quiet.

"He's asleep," Cimarron said softly.

Sarah continued to soothe him a few minutes longer, until she was sure he was slumbering soundly. "There are linens in the closet. Do you know how to make a bed?" she asked Cimarron. "There's a trundle for him under the double bed."

"I can manage."

Cimarron made both beds, right down to folding hospital corners, with a practiced efficiency that made Sarah more curious about him. She carefully laid Wyatt on the clean sheets and then eased up the legs of his pajamas, looking for marks. Cimarron moved beside her.

"What are you doing?" he asked.

"Looking for some reason he would be crying like that," she said. "Spider bites, splinters..."

"Bruises, broken bones?" he finished the thought. "I didn't hurt him, if that's what you're looking for. He's afraid of the dark, and as you know, there's no electricity in that old house."

"Oh, so it's my fault?"

"He's afraid of the dark," Cimarron repeated, the sarcasm in his voice replaced by weariness. "I left him inside to answer a phone call and I guess when he woke up alone, he panicked. Go ahead and check him over. I'd like to be sure nothing bit him, too."

"Was he sleeping on the floor?"

"No, in a sleeping bag on a cot."

She gingerly moved Wyatt's pajamas around until she had finished checking him, then covered him and turned to Cimarron with her arms folded across her chest.

"Now, I want some answers."

"About what? He's not hurt. You saw that."

"Maybe not now, but he obviously isn't comfortable with you, and from the little I've seen of how you treat him you don't want him. There are too many lost and kidnapped kids out there for me to just ignore the way you two act together."

"Wait a minute—"

"No, you wait a minute. Either you explain to me why you've got this child with you, or I'll let Griff ask the questions."

"You would, wouldn't you?"

"In a heartbeat."

Cimarron huffed and ran a hand through his thick, curling hair. He walked to the door and back, then shoved his hands into his jeans pockets. "Okay, you win. It's nothing like that. I've got nothing to hide, so you might as well know. His daddy died in a construction accident last month. I'm Wyatt's legal guardian."

"Where's his mother?"

"She surrendered her parental rights when he was a baby. My brother was raising him alone."

"Grandparents?"

"Nope. I'm about all he's got left and that's not much."

"He looks enough like you to be yours."

"I know," Cimarron said, glancing at the sleeping child. "All the Cole men look alike. I was mistaken for my brother's twin all the time by strangers, even though he was four years older."

"I'm sorry to hear about the accident. So you've only had Wyatt a month?"

"Around that. I'm obviously not a fast learner in the daddy department. But he's never cried like this before. I guess, when I think about it, I haven't ever been far from him since R.J. died, and at night I'm always within reach if he wakes up. I never thought about him waking when I went outside." Cimarron looked around the room, resting his fingertips on the glowing finish of an antique side table. "Nice piece. Nice room. You keep it ready for guests all the time?"

A small furnished kitchen nestled in a niche at the back, while the front area was furnished with a sofa, a couple of chairs and a small dinette set. To the right, under a wide window, sat the double bed with an antique iron frame covered by a patchwork quilt and several plump pillows. A compact dresser with mirror stood against one wall and a lamp and alarm clock/radio combo were positioned on the bedside table. Colorful throw rugs covered polished wooden floors and local landscapes made the room feel cozy.

"My uncle's chef lived here until the fishing lodge closed. My parents visit now and then, so I keep it ready for them. I used to let Bobby stay here when he was in town, but that's history."

Cimarron wisely made no comment on Bobby. Instead he said, "You can go back to bed. I'll stay with Wyatt the rest of the night and clear out of here first thing in the morning."

"Out of Little Lobo?" Sarah asked hopefully.

"No, out of your apartment."

"Figures," she muttered. "I'll stay a while longer. How about a cup of coffee?"

She didn't want to leave the child until she knew he'd recovered from his fright. Cimarron looked pretty ragged, too, and her nurturing instinct couldn't help but peek out from its hidey-hole. That part of her, once on almost constant call for brother, Bobby, wasn't needed very often anymore.

"Sure, I'd love one."

Sarah moved into the kitchen, taking a kettle from a cabinet beside the stove and filling it with water. She busied herself making the coffee, grinding beans from her mother's private stash in the refrigerator, but her mind was still on the small boy who was scared out of his wits by the darkness and crying for his daddy. She couldn't bring his daddy back, but she could do one thing for him.

She turned to Cimarron, studying his tired face. "I don't want you to take this the wrong way..." She hesitated. Should she offer or not? It might open a new can of worms, hurt her attempt to get her house back. Then the child whimpered in his sleep, and she gave in. "I'm going to offer to let you stay in this room—"

"You don't have to do that. We'll be all right."

"Trust me, I'm not doing it for you. And nothing between us has changed. I still want my house back. But I don't want him to be scared or cold out there because you're too damn stubborn to go to a motel."

"It was full."

"Whatever. Just stay here, for his sake. You won't be here that long anyway."

Cimarron laughed. "You sound pretty sure."

Sarah frowned at him. "One way or another."

"We'll see how it works out. Anyway, thanks for the offer of the room. I'll take it, for Wyatt. How much do you want?"

"For what?"

"Rent. I'm not going to take advantage of your hospitality."

"A million and a half for a week."

He sighed and shook his head. "That's a little steep. How about two hundred a night."

"That's really more than it's worth."

"Not to me. I'm ready for a hot shower. 'Course, for that price, I normally get room service." He grinned and his teasing eyes grew darker, if that was possible.

How could any man have such a stunning smile? She firmed her resolve and gave him a withering look. "Not on your life."

"Okay, fine, it was worth a try. Where are the cups?"

Sarah indicated one of the cupboards. "All I have here are dry creamer and sugar packets in that dish by the stove."

She poured the freshly brewed coffee into mugs and carried them to the table. Cimarron brought along the creamer and sugar and took the chair across the table from her. She noticed that he drank his coffee black, just as she did. Dark hair, thick and unruly, had fallen over his tanned forehead and curled down the nape of his neck. Arched eyebrows made him appear a bit cynical when he looked up and caught her staring. Then he smiled. She was beginning to look forward to that gorgeous smile, which exposed white teeth that appeared to be naturally straight with just enough imperfection to make her suspect they'd never seen braces.

"You make excellent coffee," he said. He leaned back, his hands cupped loosely around the mug. "I noticed that the other morning in the café. Reminds me of the coffee in Louisiana, where they hit it with a little chicory."

Sarah smiled. "I'm impressed. It is a special New Orleans blend with chicory. Are you from Louisiana?"

"No. Idaho, originally. But my last project was a plantation house in south Louisiana. Hot as hell down there in the summer."

"Oh, I saw that home on your Web page. Impressive, again. You do excellent work."

"Why, thank you. I try. This house will turn out just as well. It has good bones, so to speak." Sarah's face fell, and Cimarron wished he'd kept his mouth shut.

"Let's not go there tonight, if you don't mind. I'm too tired to be depressed."

"Why don't you get some sleep. I'll leave the light on in here, in case Wyatt wakes again."

Sarah glanced at the clock on the bedside table: 3:00 a.m. "No need to go to bed now. I have to be up in an hour in order to get ready for breakfast."

"I'm sorry we woke you, but I really appreciate your help. I don't know that I would ever have gotten him quiet until the sun came up."

"He'd have cried himself out sooner or later."

"Later. He doesn't respond to me like he did to you. As if he trusted you. Of course, he's got no reason to trust me, really. He hardly knows me."

"You're his uncle. Why doesn't he know you?"

Cimarron shrugged. "Long, boring story. Dysfunctional family. I'd only seen Wyatt once before R.J. begged a job off me and brought Wyatt along. Then he...he was killed and I found out he'd made me Wyatt's guardian."

"Without telling you?"

"I imagine he knew I'd kick up a fuss. Besides, he didn't have anybody else."

"Guess you'll have to alter your lifestyle now."

Cimarron rubbed a hand across his mouth but said nothing. He took a swallow of coffee and stared past her at Wyatt.

"Something's going to have to change," he said. "No doubt about that."

CHAPTER TEN

WYATT OPENED his eyes to a mere slit, not sure where he was. He'd never lain on anything so soft. Maybe it was a cloud. He looked around the shining white room, with its yellow curtains and the sweet smell of outdoors wafting in through the screen door. Panic inched up his body. Where was he? Was he alone? Where was Unca—

He sat upright, staring around wildly, then breathed a sigh of relief. His uncle slept in a chair nearby. Wyatt eased back under the downy covers, cocooned in warmth and security, pondering the dream he'd had the night before.

He'd been in his mother's arms. She'd rubbed his back and told him not to be afraid. Then she'd sung the most beautiful song. He couldn't remember her face, but that didn't surprise him. He'd never seen his real mother—at least not since he could remember stuff. But the mother who held him last night had soft, glowing hair and a gentle, sweet voice, and she smelled good.

He closed his eyes, hoping to dream the dream again, but he couldn't get back to sleep. He had to go to the bathroom, but he didn't know where the Porta Potti was. Besides he was afraid if he got out of bed and wakened his uncle, this wonderful new room would vanish just like the mother in his dream. He tried to lie still, but the urge to pee grew stronger and he fidgeted until he couldn't wait any longer. He was going to have to find the Porta Potti or wake his uncle and ruin everything.

Cimarron heard the rustle of bedcovers and opened his eyes. Wyatt slid gingerly from the bed, tiptoeing across the rugs on the wooden floor, looking around urgently.

"Where are you going?" Cimarron said.

Wyatt jumped and stared at him, as if he might vanish. "I gotta go to the bathroom and I don't know where the potty is."

"Through that door." Cimarron pointed. "A real one."

Wyatt went in, did his business and came out again. "Wow. Is this a motel room?"

"No, this is an apartment attached to Sarah's café. She said we could stay here for a few days. Is that all right with you?"

"You bet!"

Wyatt looked happier than he had since he'd been with Cimarron. Actually, Cimarron was happier than he'd been in the past few weeks, too. Sarah's appearance in the middle of the night couldn't have been more welcome. Talking to her about Wyatt had lightened his burden somewhat and he looked forward to seeing her again this morning.

"How about we clean up for breakfast?" After Wyatt bathed, Cimarron took a quick, hot shower, which did wonders for his constitution. As the steaming water pelted his skin, he said a little thank-you to Wyatt for being afraid of the dark.

Several cars and two big rigs sat in the café parking lot, and the place was hopping when Cimarron and Wyatt sat down inside. Cimarron ordered eggs, biscuits, sausage and coffee. Wyatt wanted pancakes and strawberries. A rough-complexioned young man could be seen at regular intervals, placing dishes under the warming lights of the pass-through from the kitchen. Sarah worked the tables cheerfully in spite of the dark circles under her eyes, her bright smile and easy chatter in stark contrast to the look Cimarron usually got from her.

After last night, he found himself watching her closely as she worked. Jeans snugged her butt just as his hand itched to do, and her well-worn cowboy boots looked as if they had two-stepped around a dance floor a few times. A pale pink polo-style shirt complemented her creamy complexion and the shining red curls piled on her head.

Pink might become his favorite color, since the whole café was decorated in pink with the exception of white chairs and the white shutters that could be folded back during daytime to let in light and closed at night for privacy. On the other hand, maybe he could lend her some advice on café decor and get rid of the pink vinyl booths that lined the walls and the pink checkered cloths that covered the tables.

In spite of their differences, he was beginning to like her. She was being very kind to Wyatt this morning, and she even favored Cimarron with a couple of small smiles that made his insides flutter. Even better, her helper cooked Cimarron's breakfast to perfection.

Harry Upshaw bellied up to the counter. "Well, good morning, little lady. I'll just have my usual."

Sarah set a glass of juice on the counter and poured a steaming cup of coffee. The bulky man took a swig of the hot coffee without flinching. Within minutes, she placed a platter before him, loaded with three eggs, four sausage patties and two large, fluffy biscuits alongside a large helping of hash browns. He immediately set to, talking as he chewed. No wonder the old guy's shirt buttons were about to pop over his middle.

"I brought you a standard boilerplate contract, since you want one so bad, and a rough estimate of materials and all. Like I said, I can't give you to-the-penny. Might run into complications. Did you get them latches on the doors Sunday?"

Sarah tried to get a word in as he rumbled on, mouth full, without paying her any attention. Cimarron wanted to take that proverbial two-by-four to the old coot's forehead and make him a little more courteous. Instead, he kept quiet and listened. It was Sarah's ball game, at this point, unless she told the contractor to begin work.

"I thought if you sign these this morning I could bring in some men to work on the roof. The sooner we get started, the sooner you've got your new business going."

Sarah glanced at Cimarron, no smile this time. Her lips drew into a fine line and she looked back at Harry. "About that, Harry. I...I'm going to have to postpone the project."

Harry stopped midchew. "What you talking about? We have an agreement."

"I know, but, well, I've run into a problem with the title."

"Where's Bobby? I'll get this straight with him."

Cimarron sensed Sarah's rising ire. "Bobby's done enough. It's my problem and I'll solve it. When I do, I'll get back to you. Hopefully later this week."

"That's not going to cut bait, Miss Sarah. How come you're backing out? You planning on hiring that newcomer with the fancy truck, instead of me?"

"No, certainly not. It's a problem with the deed, like I explained. I'm sorry," Sarah said with finality. "There's just nothing I can do until I get the title free and clear."

"And I'm sorry, too. 'Cause my time's been wasted and now I'm going to have to try to get one of those other jobs back." He pushed away the empty plate. "And you'll just have to get in line till I'm free again."

A hurt look crossed Sarah's face and she bit her lower lip. Cimarron's blood boiled. The old SOB. He didn't have to be hateful—he'd just lost any chance of working on that house. Cimarron made himself a promise to see to that. And he wanted Sarah to smile again. He hadn't meant to bring her world down around her and he wished he could make it right. Somehow.

The few customers still in the café watched Harry walk out, then stared at Sarah. Embarrassed, she gave a tentative smile and a shrug and ducked into the kitchen for a couple of minutes. When she came out she was composed and soon she had everyone ticketed, paid and out the door. All except Cimarron. She took one quick, scathing glance at him and returned to the kitchen.

He laid enough money on the counter to pay for his meal and cover a generous tip and left before she came back. For the next hour he and Wyatt relocated everything from the house, except the lantern and cots. When that was done, he left the outer door to the tiny apartment open to allow cool air in through the screen. He laid his cell phone and wallet on the table and took his laptop from a case sitting next to the door.

Without a word, Wyatt found his coloring book and crayons and lay down on the floor in a square of sunshine streaming through the door.

A peaceful quiet settled over the room and Cimarron let the work he loved consume him. Ideas tumbled over one another and he strove to get them all down. The rooms he created were beautiful, planned to the most minute detail.

Once in a while he glanced at Wyatt, who filled the pages of the thick coloring book as fast as he could. He might not know his numbers or his alphabet, but the kid was a whiz with crayons.

A talented software writer had written the design program for Cimarron's business according to his specs, and nothing else on the market could touch it for power, depth or versatility. That one program often gave him an edge on bids. Not only could he produce floor plans, plumbing and electrical diagrams, complete rooms, but he could enhance the renderings until they resembled photographs. There was even a three-hundred-sixty-degree virtual-tour option.

Over the clicking of the keyboard, he could hear sounds of activity coming through the walls from the café on the other side. Around ten o'clock, he heard Aaron tell Sarah goodbye, followed by the crunch of tires leaving the parking lot.

As Cimarron worked, troubling thoughts about Wyatt's future swirled through his mind. The boy needed to be in school. He needed a home that didn't move on four wheels and a real bed to sleep in every night. He needed a loving mom waiting for him when he came home from school, with warm cookies and cold milk, ready to discuss all the highlights and problems of his day. A dad who had time to play baseball and football with him. Teach him to hunt and fish. One who could comfort him in the middle of a dark night.

Cimarron's hands stilled on the keyboard, his gaze fixed on the screen. All the things he couldn't be to Wyatt. If the lawyer didn't find him a good home fast, Cimarron would have to try one of the adoption agencies. The longer the child was kept in limbo, the harder the transition would be—for both of them.

Yet if the lawyer found an adoptive family tomorrow, Wyatt would be blindsided again, his world yanked from under his feet. Cimarron had to have that dreaded talk with him beforehand. Today? When all was quiet and peaceful. He looked hesitantly at Wyatt, whose face was drawn into a serious frown as he filled in a space on his picture.

"Wyatt?" Cimarron said, pretending to continue his work, which was a hopeless cause right now with this on his mind. "How's the coloring coming along?"

"Fine. How's your stuff coming along?"

Cimarron gave a soft chuckle. "Just fine. I was thinking about how we're going to get you into school."

Wyatt's crayon stilled. "I don't want to go to school."

"You have to. It's a law. Maybe not right now, but soon. And you need to. They'll teach you your ABCs and numbers and how to read for yourself."

"Don't you know all those things, Unca Cimron?"

"Well...yeah."

"Then why can't you teach me?"

"I can teach you some, but I'm not as good as a real teacher. And I wouldn't have time to teach you much, since I have to work all day."

Wyatt didn't comment.

"Anyway, I was thinking about another problem."

"What?" Wyatt asked softly.

"If we enroll you in school here, then when I finish this house and get another one someplace else, you'll have to change schools. In fact, every time I change jobs you'll have to leave your school friends behind. I'm not sure that's a good idea."

"I don't need no friends."

Cimarron couldn't argue that point with him, since he'd called very few people "friend" over his own lifetime. "You still have to go to school. That's a rule. Kids have to go to school."

"Well, I reckon I could do school if I had to. But I don't want no friends."

"What I was thinking about is this. There are lots of nice families out there who'd really like to have a little boy. Families with a mom and a dad and maybe brothers and sisters. They live in a house and don't move all over..."

"Don't want one," Wyatt said firmly, sitting upright and putting down his crayon.

"You don't want a mom to take care of you and—"

"Never had a mom. Don't need one."

Cimarron turned to him. "You'd be part of a family, Wyatt. A real family." *Like I never had. Like you can't imagine.*

Wyatt narrowed his eyes, folded his arms across his chest and shook his head. "My daddy told me him and you were the only family I'd ever need."

"But that was before..." Cimarron struggled for the words to make the child understand. "I'm not...I—"

"Hello, may I come in?" Sarah knocked lightly as she spoke.

Wyatt jumped up to stand behind Cimarron's chair.

"Sure, come in."

"Am I interrupting anything?"

"No, not really. I think Wyatt was tired of talking, anyway." He wondered how much of their conversation she had overheard.

Sarah stepped into the room, glancing around as if they might have trashed it already. "I wanted to check and see how Wyatt was doing today," Sarah said. "I didn't get a chance to really talk to you in the café this morning."

"Looks like you turn a good business for breakfast."

"Not bad." She made a pretense of stretching her neck to see Wyatt behind Cimarron. "Are you okay this morning, Wyatt?"

• • • •

Wyatt nodded, astounded. It was his mother's voice...from the dream. And the shining hair. A whiff of her perfume reached his nose. And the way she smelled. His dream mother...was Sarah!

Cimarron reached around and caught him by the waist, gently prodding him to come forward from his hiding place.

"This nice room with lights belongs to Sarah. You need to thank her for letting us stay here."

Pushing back against the pressure of the arm at his back, Wyatt unwillingly moved around to stand beside Cimarron's knee.

"Thank you," he said, ducking his head. Could she see how hard his heart was beating? Did she know she was his dream mother?

"You're welcome. Do you remember when I brought you here last night?"

Wyatt nodded. She did know! "You rubbed my back and sang a pretty song."

Sarah smiled.

"That's right," she said. "Do you like it here with lights?"

"Yes. Unca Cimron said we didn't have to move back to the old house," he ventured. Now he wanted to stay in this room forever.

"That's right. I told him you could live here for a while."

Her gaze moved from Wyatt to linger on the open laptop on the table and she gave a slight shake of her head, the smile fading. She and Uncle Cimarron didn't get along very well. That wasn't good. If they argued, Sarah might make them leave, like Erica had done with his daddy. *Please, don't make her mad, Unca Cimron. Please!*

• • • •

"Want to see?" Cimarron asked. He didn't want that pretty smile to go away. Maybe if she saw what he intended to do...

"I don't think so," Sarah said.

"Sure you do." Cimarron turned in his seat and slid the laptop around on the table so she could see better, then touched a key. The screen sprang to life. He clicked again and displayed a full size architectural rendering of a cozy room flanked by floor-to-ceiling windows, with a cheery fire in the fireplace beneath an intricately carved mantel.

She frowned, and then recognition dawned. "That's the parlor in the old house."

"Yes. The way it will look when I'm finished."

"How did you do that?" she asked, staring at the image on the screen.

"Long years of practice." He was rewarded by a slight upturn of the lips that might pass for a smile.

Sarah looked and absorbed. "Impressive."

"You see, it's possible," he said.

"I already knew that," she said miserably. "I saw your Web site. I have no doubt you can do exactly what you claim. Sad that you won't get the chance."

"Do you really believe you can raise that much money in such a short time?"

"I'm going to do my level best."

"Unless you've got a pot of gold somewhere that your brother Bobby missed out on, I'd say you're going to end up jeopardizing your café. And then not have enough money left to renovate the house."

"Harry will work with me."

"Harry'll ruin the integrity of that beautiful house, especially if he's doing it on the cheap."

"It doesn't have to be perfect. It just has to function as a bed-and-breakfast."

Cimarron bit his tongue to keep from lambasting her on that one. He spent his life making grand old homes like this perfect again. The thought that she was prepared to ruin it with shoddy workmanship was beyond his comprehension. He rose and walked to the screen door, staring at the house on the hill, which waited, like some wounded creature, to be made right again. He turned to Sarah.

"Don't you understand? You'll damage it beyond repair. Right now it can be restored pretty much to the original state. If you let Harry Upshaw in there, bashing away, you'll mess up something that's irreplaceable. The essence of this old house. Once it's gone, you won't be able to get it back...Like a lot of things in life."

She studied his face intently. "Such as?"

"Such as...things you don't value enough until they're lost." Like a mother he couldn't save and a brother who was trying to do the right thing by his son.

"Why does this falling-down old place mean so much to you?" she asked, her expression one of total bewilderment.

Cimarron stared at her, then shook his head slightly. "You probably wouldn't understand."

"I do understand. You want to make a killing off the restoration by selling my house to strangers. And I'm the one who's going to have to live beside them and watch other people living my dream and there'll be nothing I can do about it!"

Her words stung. Not what he wanted at all, that vision she had conjured. He knew too well how it felt to watch others living the life you wanted for yourself. He caught her by the arms without thinking. "Sarah, I never meant that to happen. I just didn't know. And now your brother's blown that money to hell and back."

"So I have to come up with it," she said. "Of course, that little extra you tagged on doesn't help."

"It's a fair price. I can't just blink away my investment."

"Well, like you said, I can't afford to pay that price and still do all this fancy restoration you're talking about. But if the house serves my purpose and makes me happy, then it's doing its job."

Cimarron frowned. Something about her words was giving him pause, but he couldn't quite identify what it was that troubled him.

"You're going to hack it up so that it can't be put right again."

"It won't be your problem, will it?"

Cimarron released her arms. "I guess not."

Silky hair curled around her face and he almost reached to brush it back before he caught himself. Her slender build made her look taller than she was and now that she stood close to him he realized the difference in their heights—she barely topped his shoulders. He caught a whiff of her subtle perfume and the clean fragrance of her hair as she looked up at him with shining eyes that left him weak in the knees.

"I wish this had never happened," she said.

He wondered if she could hear his heart hammering against his ribs. Oh, this was not good. Not good at all, the electric current running under his skin, skittering through his body, bringing him alive in more ways than one. Did he wish it had never happened? He wasn't so sure now. Sarah might hate him, but she sure was sexy. He wanted to smile when she got angry and fussed at him, but this sadness on her face...That just tempted him to kiss her worries away.

"Who knows? Maybe the man of your dreams will buy it and move in."

She narrowed her eyes at him. "There is no man in my dreams."

"Well, that's a crying shame. A woman, then?"

She gave him a light slap on the chest, her hand lingering there. Pure fire shot through him.

"No. I didn't mean that. I just don't need a man in my life, even as a neighbor."

"You never know until you try," he said, easing a fraction closer to her.

"I'm going to get my house back and then what I do with it will be my business."

The rock-solid muscle beneath her palm made Sarah think twice about not needing a man. It would be nice to have strong arms to hold her when she was tired, somebody to share her dreams and plans, an understanding embrace when her day had gone bad. The thought of sharing everything with Cimarron Cole sent a rush of heat through her, made her fingers tingle where they touched his warm shirt.

She cut those thoughts short. It wouldn't be this man, no matter how enticing he was. Besides, a man this drop-dead handsome would have more than his share of women flinging themselves at him, and she'd had enough of that with Griff, who only *thought* he was God's gift to womankind.

Cimarron reached around her, powered down the laptop and closed the cover. Then he braced his rigid arms on the table edge on either side of her waist, effectively trapping her. Sarah's eyes widened and she caught her breath in apprehension. Surely he wouldn't. She tried to push away one of his arms, but it was like trying to move a steel beam. He pressed against her just slightly and the sensation of his taut body so close to hers sent the simmer in her gut into a merry boil. He leaned forward until their noses almost touched and his warm breath tickled her face.

"Well, Sarah," he said softly, his voice rumbling through her body as his dark-lashed eyes bored into hers. "I guess we'll just have to wait and see what happens."

"Unca Cimron, are you going to kiss Sarah like my daddy kissed Erica?"

Cimarron jumped away as if he'd been scalded. Sarah fought back a smile.

"No, he's not going to kiss Sarah at all," she said.

"My daddy tried to kiss Erica a lot."

"Must run in the family," Sarah said, moving to the door.

"Sometimes Erica hit him when he tried."

Sarah arched an eyebrow at Cimarron. "Not a bad idea. I'll keep that in mind next time."

Cimarron reached down to clamp a hand over Wyatt's mouth. "There won't be a next time," he said to Wyatt, then shot a grin to Sarah. "Unless Sarah kisses me."

Sarah's mouth fell open, a retort on her lips, but she couldn't get it out. Instead, she spun around and marched out the door.

"Go color, Wyatt," Cimarron ordered, following Sarah. "Hey, wait," he called as she stormed across the yard to the café. He caught up to her halfway there. "I didn't mean anything by that."

"Just don't try it again."

"Like I said, unless you kiss me."

Sarah bristled. "Oooh, like I would...would—"

"Kiss me? Hey, you might like it."

She prepared to tear into him again, but he put his hands up in defense.

"Don't hit me, I'm just kidding. I wanted to tell you I'm going to start working on the house while we see if you can come up with the money."

"No!" she said. "You'll charge me for what you do, and I can't afford it."

"The house needs to be made watertight, no matter who does the work. I'm just going to get that done before it rains again."

"I'll get Harry to do it."

"Nope. I don't want him touching that house as long as I own it. I won't charge you any more than he would, and I'll do it right. I've got to have something to do. I can't just sit around."

"You could go away," Sarah snapped. Then she left him standing and rushed into the café through the back door.

In her office, she flung herself into her chair. Deep inside she was afraid that Cimarron was right. Even if she managed to buy her house back, she wouldn't be able to remodel it for a long, long time—maybe never.

Yet Cimarron could restore it to its original grandeur. He could make it beautiful, functional...perfect. Then he would sell it for a fortune and she'd have to live beside it for a lifetime, knowing it would never belong to her family again.

"It's just not fair," she muttered.

Feeling sorry for herself only wasted time. She squared her shoulders, found a notepad and pencil, and began jotting down names of people who might be able to help her. Jon and Kaycee Rider were possibilities, but even though Kaycee had offered to help all she could, Sarah couldn't exactly ask for a million dollars as a favor. And Jon and Kaycee were the richest people she knew. Well, except maybe Cimarron Cole—as if she could ask him to finance her house.

Once she had drawn up a list of people to contact, she worked on an introductory pitch. Opening a spreadsheet on her computer, she typed in Harry's cost estimate line by line. This was the first time she'd had a chance to look at the numbers. Even with Harry doing the work, fixing up the old house would be expensive.

The enormity and hopelessness of her situation hit her full force. What had she done to deserve this from her brother? Nothing. Not a darned thing.

She picked up the phone and dialed a number, holding the receiver on her shoulder as she jotted notes beside the names on her list. When she heard the familiar voice on the other end, she said, "Mom? Has Bobby told you what he did?"

Half an hour later, Sarah hung up, her world somewhat stabilized by the unconditional support of her mom and dad. At least Bobby would get another earful. Dad swore Bobby would be selling that "damn RV" and sending the money to her, but she dared not count on that until she saw the greenbacks in her hand. Online, she checked her own savings account—again. Not surprisingly, the balance had not increased since yesterday. She dreaded more than anything calling on her friends and business associates for money.

With a loud sigh, she dialed the number at the top of her list—the banker who had lent her the money to modernize the café after her uncle died.

CHAPTER ELEVEN

SO MUCH HAD to be done just to protect the old house from further damage before Cimarron could even begin to bring it back. Starting upstairs, he worked his way slowly through the interior, making detailed notes on an electronic notepad while Wyatt followed him step for step with his own old-fashioned clipboard and a pencil.

Cimarron lost track of time as he inspected every inch of the place, uncovering hidden damage in some places but finding pleasant surprises in others. Lovely detailed woodwork still in excellent condition. Enough original wallpaper hidden under the top layers that Cimarron would be able to match or duplicate it. He whistled softly as he worked in his element.

The little shadow that followed him, scribbling away, served as a constant reminder of the changes wrought in their lives over the past few weeks. R.J. had truly loved his son. He hadn't left five-year-old Wyatt to fend for himself on purpose—but he'd given Cimarron a lot more credit than warranted by trusting him with the child's welfare. The boy didn't deserve to be stuck with a clueless vagabond, jerked from place to place, farmed out to babysitters or day-care workers during the long hours Cimarron was on the job.

Cimarron tried to envision the perfect family for Wyatt. He couldn't. His own family had been anything *but* perfect, as far back as Cimarron could recall. His dad, Jackson, had been gone from home so long at a time that young Cimarron often forgot what he looked like between visits. His brother took off at sixteen to follow Jackson around the rodeo circuit, leaving twelve-year-old Cimarron behind with their mother, whose health problems steadily worsened over the years, aggravated by the stress of abject poverty and her concern for her young son, who took the burden of her care squarely on his shoulders.

Cimarron had no memories of carefree afternoons playing with friends, staying overnight, or having them to his house. Hell, he'd never had any friends. And no idea how a real family interacted. All he had to rely on were the old sitcoms his mother loved to watch—*Leave It To Beaver* and *The Dick Van Dyke Show*. A loving mother in pearls, cooking, cleaning a huge, beautiful house, and a father who came home from work every day and took a keen interest in his sons.

Cimarron had never wanted to be like his daddy, in any way. And he never, not once—until R.J. died—thought he had an ounce of his daddy in him. That rotten DNA that had made Jackson Cole turn his back on his family's needs and blithely load up his saddle, his horses and his older son and ride off to the next rodeo, leaving responsibility behind. Now Cimarron knew better, and it tore at him every minute of those long days that he spent trying to decide what would be best for Wyatt.

He clenched the pen so hard that his hand trembled and he had to wait for the tremor to pass before he could write again. Get your mind off it, he told himself, but the dilemma crouched there in the back of his mind ready to spring the instant he dropped his guard.

A tug on his pant leg caught his attention. "What?" he said without looking down.

"That dog's here," Wyatt whispered.

"What dog?"

"That one that ran off with your coat at the stream."

Cimarron jerked around in time to see a furry brown head disappear around the door frame in the foyer. He rushed to the other room, but the dog was gone. "Good riddance."

"I think it likes us," Wyatt said optimistically.

"Too bad. Don't you touch it. It probably bites."

"Okay." The edge of disappointment cut, but there was no need for Wyatt to get attached to a stray that would likely run off in a few days. The slant of the sun's rays made him glance at his watch. Well past noon.

"Let's break for lunch."

"Okay."

Since Sarah hadn't kicked them out of the apartment yet, Cimarron had bought a few groceries—so they wouldn't have to eat in the café every meal. Not so much to save money, as to avoid seeing Sarah, knowing that she truly despised him. He wished they had met under better circumstances, because he didn't despise her at all. Far from it. Another empty wish.

He and Wyatt took sandwiches and chips back to the house and sat on the steps to eat.

"So, did you make some notes today?" Cimarron asked, trying to come up with some sort of conversation to engage the five-year-old.

"Yep, lots."

"That's good. Let's see what you've got."

Wyatt held up his clipboard. Several pages were filled with chicken scratches since Wyatt had no idea how to write, but the pictures he'd drawn impressed Cimarron. Or maybe all five-year-olds could draw that well. How would he know?

"I wrote down what color to paint the walls, and what color the floor is and stuff like that."

"What color for the walls?" Right now they were a dirty tan plaster.

"Well," Wyatt said with all seriousness, "they're not real pretty the way they are, but there's some paint under that brown that's kinda reddish-yellow that I liked."

"Really?" Cimarron had noticed that color, too, but he'd had no idea Wyatt could catch it. "There was a green color under the layers, too. Did you see that one?"

Wyatt nodded. "I didn't like it much, but I've got one in my color box that I do like."

He jumped up and ran down the slope to the apartment, reappearing a minute later, crayons in hand. Breathless, he sat down close to Cimarron and pulled out a crayon.

"This one is my favorite."

Cimarron took the crayon and studied it. "Nice. Do you know the name of this color?" Cimarron pointed to the name written on the side.

"No, I can't read the words."

"Yellow-green."

"It doesn't look yellow to me."

"If there are two colors listed, the last color will be stronger. That's why it looks more like green. It's a good color for the walls."

"I like this color, too. What's it called?" Wyatt handed him another crayon.

"Raw sienna. Sienna's a brown color. Raw means it's in its pure form." Cimarron took his turn to pull out a crayon. "This one is burnt sienna. The sienna clay is heated and it turns more reddish."

"Wow," Wyatt said, comparing the two crayons. Carefully he put them back and slid another crayon out. "What's this color, Unca Cimron?"

"Sea green."

"I like it for the walls, too," Wyatt said.

"So do I. We'll have to see if that was a color the people would have had years ago when the house was built."

"Are we going to live in this house after it's fixed?" Wyatt asked, rolling a crayon over and over between his fingers.

"No. I bought it so I could fix it and sell it."

"Who are you going to sell it to?"

Cimarron shrugged. "I don't know. Sarah wants it, but I don't know if she'll buy it."

"Maybe we could live here with her."

Cimarron gave a short bark of a laugh. "Somehow I don't think so. I didn't think you liked this house, anyway."

"I like it better than I did before. What's this color called?"

One after the other, Wyatt took the crayons from the box and Cimarron identified them. To Cimarron's surprise, when he picked out crayons later, Wyatt could name each one of them. Cimarron leaned back on his elbows on the steps and Wyatt copied him.

"You really like to color, don't you?" he asked Wyatt.

"Yep, 'bout my favorite thing. Thanks for the big box of colors, Unca Cimron. I've never seen so many pretty colors."

Cimarron grunted. He'd never seen so many pretty crayons in one box either. "Guess we'd better get on to the kitchen, huh?"

"That dog's back again," Wyatt said quietly, pointing.

Soulful eyes stared at them from the corner of the house. The scruffy brown mutt was thin and dirty.

"It's hungry, Unca Cimron. Can't we give it the rest of my sandwich?"

"No. If we feed her, she'll just hang around. She might bite, or she could be sick."

"I think she's just dirty."

"You mind me, and don't feed her or try to pet her. Understand?"

"Okay."

They rose to go back to work. Wyatt picked up his clipboard and crayon box and ran inside. Cimarron gave the dog a sidelong look. She whined and her mouth opened into a wide dog grin. Cimarron scowled at her, but as he walked into the house he tossed her the remaining fragment of Wyatt's sandwich.

From the back door of the café, Sarah watched Cimarron disappear into the house. The old phrase about attracting more flies with honey than vinegar came to mind and Sarah pondered the wisdom of being sweet as sugar to Cimarron Cole until she got what she wanted. Maybe she could even get to him through that young nephew of his, as much as that might gall her.

The end would justify the means, considering the mortification she was enduring with each phone call she made. So far, not so good. Between her own life savings, the help her parents could provide and a standing offer from Kaycee and Jon Rider to cosign a substantial loan with her, she could come up with about half the amount she needed. Bobby was being a horse's butt about selling the RV, so she couldn't count on anything from him.

Thoroughly discouraged, she retreated to her office to spend her free time making more ingratiating calls. She hated begging, hated being dependent on anybody. Hated Cimarron Cole for putting her in this position.

Being nice to him would test every fiber of her being. If it weren't for the child, she'd turn him out of her apartment, too. But the little boy seemed sad and lost and afraid of the dark, and she didn't have the heart.

That idea about buttering up Cimarron looked better and better as the days passed and she made scant progress toward her goal. She tried every bank in Montana, and got the same answer from all of them. Her café wasn't sufficient collateral for that large a loan, and the old building wasn't worth restoring. All this without looking at the café *or* the building. She wondered if Cimarron could call any banker anywhere and get a loan for twice that on his say-so. He looked the type. And he had the reputation. Too bad he wasn't getting the loan for her.

She'd seen him coming and going several times, and he'd had a load of building materials delivered. Tomorrow was Sunday. Maybe in the afternoon she'd just check out the old house and remind him that she was not going to pay for any of his supplies.

On Sunday, Sarah went to church as soon as she and Aaron finished cleanup after breakfast. Jon and Kaycee were there with the kids, and afterward the adults discussed Sarah's situation. Jon wanted to look at the house. Sarah understood Jon's reasoning, even though it worried her that he might back out of helping her if he actually saw the place.

He was, after all, a businessman, and he wouldn't likely finance a hopeless venture. She just didn't know how cooperative Cimarron would be.

She had a plan, though, and after church she changed into jeans and a rugby shirt and went up the hill. She found Cimarron in the parlor, ripping out a rotten baseboard from under the windows. From the pile of debris she'd seen outside, he must have had to remove quite a bit of bad wood from the house.

Wyatt perched on the hearth, leaning over an open book, coloring away. Sarah moved close enough to see the picture of a cowboy that he was working on. He glanced around, saw her and sat bolt upright, an uneasy look on his face.

"Hi, Wyatt," she said.

"Hey," he said.

Cimarron twisted around to look at her, then rose and pulled off his work gloves. "Hello," he said. "Haven't seen you much this week."

"I've been busy," she said. Recalling her determination to be nice to him, she resisted smarting off that she'd had a lot more free time before he came along. "So, what exactly are you doing in here? I hope you don't think I'm going to pay you for all this."

"I doubt that's going to be a big issue."

She saw the seriousness in his dark eyes. He wasn't making fun of her, just stating a fact, but it hurt her feelings.

"Don't get too wrapped up in this house."

"The work I'm doing is just prep work. You'll have to get it done anyway."

"I am not paying you for all that lumber outside, either. I didn't agree to buying any supplies."

"Look, Sarah, don't worry about it. Is that what you came up here for?"

Remember, use honey...attract the rotten fly with honey, she chanted to herself. "No, actually I came to see if you and Wyatt would like to come to the café this afternoon. My friend Kaycee, the vet next door, is bringing her kids over for milk shakes, and I thought Wyatt might like to meet the twins. They're about his age."

Wyatt had returned to his coloring, but when Sarah mentioned milk shakes he glanced at Cimarron, as if trying to gauge his uncle's reaction. This would not be a child who pitched a fit to get his way. Quite the opposite, he might be too compliant.

"Do you like milk shakes, Wyatt?" she asked.

"Yes'um. I like them fine."

"Good." She gave Cimarron a look. "So why don't you come to the café around two."

"I don't want to butt in," he said.

Sarah laughed. "Trust me, one more won't make a difference. You guys might enjoy it."

Cimarron thought about it a moment, then glanced at Wyatt and back to her. "Sure, why not. I love milk shakes."

Sarah noticed Wyatt, bent low over his coloring book, pressing his lips together and trying to keep a neutral face. She suspected he liked milk shakes better than his uncle did. "Good. See you then."

. . . .

After Sarah left, Cimarron put his tools away, wondering what the woman had up her sleeve, too skeptical to believe she was inviting him and Wyatt to her party purely out of goodwill.

"Let's go clean up, Wyatt, if you want to have that milk shake."

"You want one, too. Don't you?"

Cimarron knew the kid well enough by now to understand what he was really asking: *You're not going to leave me there alone, are you?* "Sure, I want one, too. I hope Sarah's shakes are as good as her breakfasts."

"Me, too. What kids did she mean?"

"I guess that lady vet next door has some. We'll see. Get your things together and let's go."

Cimarron had seen the woman vet several times, along with another young woman who gave riding lessons in the afternoon, although he'd never had occasion to speak to either of them. As far as kids? He hadn't paid any attention to that, so he was surprised when he and Wyatt rounded the corner of the café a few minutes later and saw Kaycee Rider emerge from the clinic, followed by a stream of them. Cimarron's eyebrows lifted after he hit five in his count. Then a tall man in a black cowboy hat came out with a very young boy in his arms and a small girl tagging along at his heels.

"Wow," Wyatt whispered.

Thinking the same thing, Cimarron took the small hand that sought his and they lagged behind until the two adults herded the gang into the café.

What a scene! Four girls scrambled onto bar stools. Three boys, two of them twins, fought over a stool in a tiny alcove until the man settled them into a booth. Kaycee joined Sarah behind the counter to dollop ice cream into cups for the milk-shake machine.

"Cimarron Cole, Jon Rider," Sarah said, nodding to each by way of an introduction.

The men shook hands. Cimarron at once saw the favor of Jon's dark hair and blue eyes in some of the kids, but none of them looked particularly like Kaycee, who had honey hair and green eyes. He wondered how she had managed to build a career as a vet while bearing seven children. Kaycee must have noticed his confusion.

"Jon and I married last year," she said, giving him a lovely smile. "He came complete with kids."

"Ah," was all Cimarron could muster. *Brave woman.* The thought of raising *one* kid scared the hell out of him.

Kaycee's affection for the children and their father showed in her eyes, however, and when Jon looked at her Cimarron knew what was on his mind. He wondered how long it would be before baby number eight arrived on the scene.

Cimarron led Wyatt to a seat at one of the booths along the perimeter of the room. They watched the controlled chaos with interest. As Sarah finished making the milk shakes, Kaycee handed them over the counter to Jon for the eager youngsters. When she gave Jon his shake, he leaned over the counter and kissed her. The twins poked each other and giggled, their noisy play escalating until Jon sat down in the booth with them. While he didn't stop their teasing altogether, he made them lower the decibel level a notch.

Watching the young boys brought Wyatt's plight to Cimarron's mind. He was about their age. He needed friends and playmates. School and loving attention. Every day that passed meant another day that scarred Wyatt, that kept him from being carefree and happy like these children whose laughter and chatter filled the café.

Cimarron started as something cold touched his face. Sarah laughed and handed him the icy milk shake she'd just pressed to his cheek. Wyatt sucked on a strawberry shake, which Sarah must have given him while Cimarron was lost in thought.

"Hope you like chocolate. It was the only flavor of ice cream I had left," she said.

"My favorite," he said, taking the shake as she sat down beside him. "Thanks."

He took a long pull and savored the richness of the drink. "Good milk shake," he said. "Almost as good as your coffee."

"I get a lot of practice. At both."

They both smiled at the joke.

"What about yours, Wyatt? Do you like it?"

Wyatt licked his lips. "Yum."

"Good."

"Tell her thanks for the shake, Wyatt," Cimarron said.

Between gulps that chiseled dimples into his cheeks, he said, "Thanks."

"This happen a lot? All of them coming in on Sunday? Seems like an imposition on your free afternoon."

"Not really. Kaycee's my best friend, and I've watched Jon's children grow up."

"Divorced?"

"No, his first wife, Alison, was killed in a car accident almost three years ago."

Cimarron's expression turned somber as he stared at Jon. "How'd he manage with all those little ones?"

"What choice did he have? He did the best he could. He's a wonderful dad. Patient, strong. It was tough for him, but he found Kaycee, and it's like magic to see them so happy together."

Cimarron frowned and took another sip of milk shake. He deliberately looked away from Jon and the kids. The last thing he wanted right now was a perfect dad held up to him as an example.

As the youngsters finished their shakes, Sarah joined Kaycee cleaning up behind the counter. Jon wandered over to Cimarron's booth.

"Sarah tells me you're doing some work on her uncle's house. What condition is it in?"

Cimarron figured Jon knew that Bobby had sold the house, but since he didn't mention it Cimarron didn't either.

"It needs a lot of work, but it's salvageable."

"I haven't been inside for years. I wouldn't mind looking around in there."

"Yeah, sure."

"Cimarron and I are going to walk up to the old house," Jon called to Kaycee.

"Okay. I'm going back to the clinic after we clean up."

"I want to go, Daddy," one of the twins begged.

"Me, too," the other echoed.

"Me, too," the youngest boy chimed in.

"No, you guys stay here," Jon said. "You don't need to be running around there."

When Cimarron stood, Wyatt jumped out of the booth, immediately back in shadow mode. If he tried to leave the child behind, he'd raise a ruckus. Better to bring the other boys along. Maybe they would make friends. "Your boys are welcome to come along. I've got the inside pretty clear."

"Come on, then, boys," Jon said. The twins scampered to his side and he lifted the youngest child into his arms. "This is Bo. The twins are Zach and Tyler." He rubbed Wyatt's head. "What's your name, son? Curly?"

Wyatt ducked away. "No, it's Wyatt."

"Wyatt's a good name. Used to have a cowboy work for me named Wyatt. He could ride any wild bronc we had."

Wyatt grinned proudly. "My daddy rode broncs, too. He could ride anything. He got a fatal and now he's gone."

"A fatal?" Jon said, glancing at Cimarron.

Cimarron frowned, because Wyatt really sounded like he didn't know his daddy was dead. Maybe he'd never come out with the word, but Cimarron had thought the child understood. Explain death to a five-year-old...something else he should know how to do and didn't.

"I think he means a fatal injury."

Jon nodded slightly. "I see." To Wyatt, he said, "Sounds like he was a good bronc buster."

Wyatt nodded. "He was. Real good."

The twins ran ahead, with the adults following. Wyatt lagged behind. In spite of a nagging sense of depression, Cimarron kept up his end of the conversation and showed Jon through the house. Jon asked detailed questions about all aspects of the reconstruction, until finally Cimarron grew suspicious. On the front porch once more, Jon put Bo down with the twins and they all ran off to play.

"Go with them, Wyatt," Cimarron urged.

Wyatt shook his head and clung to Cimarron's leg.

"Shy little fella," Jon said.

"He's never really been around other kids before. He'll get over it."

"Thanks for showing me the house. Looks like it's got potential."

"I wouldn't have bought it if it didn't."

"Sarah had planned to buy this house from her brother," Jon said tersely. "I know you realize that already."

"Yes, she's made me very aware of that. And I'm sure from the questions you asked, that she's come to you for help in buying it back."

Jon gave a slight nod of acquiescence. "She's a good friend of mine and Kaycee's. We don't want to see her done badly."

Cimarron started to defend himself, but then held his silence. He didn't owe an explanation to this man. His business was with Sarah, and where she found the money to buy back the house didn't matter. If she matched his asking price, he'd wash his hands of Little Lobo and move on to the next project.

CHAPTER TWELVE

EARLY MONDAY MORNING, Sarah dressed in a business suit and heels. Her phone calls, made in time snatched between café shifts, hadn't garnered the results she'd wanted. Today she was going toe-to-toe with as many bankers and businessmen as she had to, in order to find the money she needed for her house.

By the time she pulled into her carport again midafternoon, she was exhausted and angry.

"Sorry, Sarah, but you don't have sufficient collateral."

"Sorry, Sarah, I just can't lend you that much, based on the business plan you've got. No guarantee of return on investment."

"Sorry, Sarah, even if your plans pan out, we're looking at several years before the bed-and-breakfast turns a profit."

Sorry, Sarah. Sorry, Sarah. Sorry, Sarah.

On top of everything, now her business was spread all over town, the latest gossip. Poor Sarah had lost her uncle's house. What's poor Sarah going to do now? Amazing that nobody had held a benefit or raffle for *Poor Sarah* yet.

As she got out of her SUV, she took a deep breath, inhaling the sweet fragrance of wildflowers—and sawdust. Frowning, she glanced up at the old house. Cimarron stood on one leg with the other knee braced on a board laid across two sawhorses as he sawed off the end. Muscles bunched across his back with each movement of the saw. He wore a light-colored thermal knit shirt with the sleeves rolled up, jeans and work boots, and a heavy leather tool belt was strapped across his hips.

Jon had spoken to her before he left the café yesterday. He seemed to think Cimarron was being straight, and he again offered to help her get a loan for a portion of the money. Knowing about Cimarron's restoration background, Sarah wished she could hire him to remodel the house once she got it back, but she doubted he'd hire out as a handyman. Not at any price she could afford.

She noticed Wyatt on the porch, playing alone with his toys. On a whim, she dialed Kaycee on her cell phone.

"Hi, Kaycee, are you busy?"

Just hearing Kaycee's laughter made Sarah feel better. "No more than usual. I'm baking cookies in the break room. Why don't you come visit."

"Are the twins there?"

"Yes, they just got in from day camp. Why?"

"I'd like to bring Wyatt over to play. I feel sorry for him, all alone up at that house all the time. What do you think?"

"I think it's a great idea."

Sarah hung up, hoping that Cimarron wouldn't consider her suggestion meddling. Whatever. The little boy needed to have a friend or two. Cimarron had gone inside by the time she reached the porch, but Wyatt greeted her warmly.

"Hey, Sarah."

"Hey, yourself. Are you having fun?"

He shrugged. "I guess. I'll be glad when Unca Cimron finishes working."

"Pretty boring all by yourself?"

"Sometimes."

"Dr. Kaycee's baking cookies at the clinic. I thought you might like to have some with her twins."

"I don't know. Unca Cimron might not let me."

"Let's ask him and see." She held out her hand and Wyatt took it readily.

Inside they found Cimarron hammering a board into place. They waited until he finished, then Sarah said, "Cimarron, we want to ask you something."

He turned to her, then did a double take. He pushed himself up from the floor and gave a low whistle, eyeing her from head to toe and back again. "My Lord, Sarah, you look like a million dollars."

"Well, thanks, I think. But I believe I need a million and half."

He rewarded her with a wide grin that warmed his eyes and something inside her, too.

"We can't get away from that, can we?" His gaze fell on Wyatt. "Was he bothering you? I told you to stay on the porch, Wyatt."

Wyatt's hand tightened in hers. "I was on the porch. I didn't go anywhere."

"He's fine—don't fuss! I came to get him." She told Cimarron about Kaycee's invitation. "Is it okay for him to go?"

"Do you want to go over there, Wyatt?"

Wyatt bit his lip and lifted his shoulder. "Maybe."

Cimarron gave a little nod. "I think you should go. It'll be fun. And...free cookies."

Wyatt knitted his brow and then said, "Okay."

"Come on. I'll walk you over," Sarah said. "We'll be back later."

"I look forward to it," Cimarron said, but the usual sarcasm was missing from his voice.

A tiny tickle of excitement stirred in her middle, like the very tip of a cat's tail twitching. Sarah needed to get that cat back in the cage. She couldn't afford to become distracted by this man, no matter how gorgeous he might be.

They entered the clinic through the back door and Kaycee met them in the hall.

"I'm glad you came over, Wyatt," she said. "The cookies will be ready in a few minutes. Come on, the boys are playing cars."

In Kaycee's office, the twins, Zach and Tyler, sat cross-legged on the floor zooming toy trucks around and around, crashing them together once in a while.

"Zach, Tyler, look who came to play."

Both boys jumped to their feet. "Wyatt!" Zach cried.

Wyatt squeezed Sarah's hand.

"Come on, Wyatt," Zach said. "We'll each give you a car so you'll have two."

"Okay," Wyatt said, letting go. "Which ones?"

"I'll come back for you later," Sarah told him.

He nodded. "Okay."

• • • •

At first, Wyatt watched the other two boys cautiously as he joined in their game. He had hardly ever played with other kids and he wasn't sure of the rules. But he knew how to play quietly, so he did that while they shrieked and made loud car noises and bumped their cars together amid gales of laughter. Wyatt tested laughing with them, just a soft chuckle, afraid they might tell him to shut up like his daddy often did when he got too loud.

The twins paid no attention to his laughter and one of them, the one named Tyler, even zipped his car close to Wyatt's like he was going to crash it. Wyatt wished more than anything that he would, because that would make him feel like they wanted him there. But it was Zach who said, "Roooarrrr, BANG!" and broadsided Wyatt's tiny pickup truck with his Jeep.

Zack and Tyler rolled with laughter and Wyatt took a chance. He howled with laughter and rolled back, too. Both boys jumped on him, still laughing and they tussled around the room. Wyatt hadn't been so full of joy and excitement in a very long time.

"What's going on in here?" The twins' mother stood at the door, hands on her hips. But she was smiling and the warm surge of fear subsided in Wyatt.

"We're wrassling," Zach announced. "Wyatt's a good wrassler."

Pride swelled his chest. He'd never had a friend, but he wanted this boy to be one.

"I've got snacks in the break room, if you guys want milk and cookies."

"Yay!" Tyler cried, leaping up from the floor. "Come on, let's go."

They raced down the hall, Wyatt's troubles pushed to the back of his mind for now. Sooner or later, his uncle would come for him and he'd have to go back to his quiet, worried life, but for a few minutes he'd escaped.

They settled around the table with plates of assorted cookies and big glasses of milk. He gulped the milk and wolfed down two cookies fast. Never had he tasted such sweet, delicious treats in his life.

"How about a peanut butter and jelly sandwich before you fill up on those?" Kaycee said.

His mouth full, all Wyatt could do was nod vigorously. Soon a sandwich appeared before each of the boys. Giggles, teasing, knock-knock jokes—the boys laughed and ate until all the food was gone. His stomach full and round, Wyatt felt cozy and relaxed.

Growing comfortable with this family, joy bubbled inside him and then burst out in an exuberant "Yehaw!" like he'd heard his daddy yell when something went especially well. The instant the shout escaped his lips, he regretted it. Kaycee turned from the refrigerator to look at him. The boys' eyes grew wide as they stared. Wyatt wanted to shrink until he disappeared. *Stupid, stupid. Messed up everything, you dummy.*

Laughter sprang from Zach's lips and he shouted "Yehaw!" at the top of his lungs. Tyler took up the cry and Wyatt joined in the chorus.

"Well, yehaw, yourselves," Kaycee said. "I think with all that yehawing, you fellas need to play outside."

"Let's go," Zach said. "We'll play rodeo. Do you know how to play rodeo, Wyatt?"

"I think so," he said, even though he really didn't. He'd figure it out.

"Cool. Come on."

As he followed the boys outside, Wyatt remembered his uncle Cimarron's questions the other night about going to live with a new family. The thought was scary because he'd never known anybody but his daddy and his uncle and a few of his daddy's girlfriends. But if a new family could be like this, it might not be so bad. Everything sure was nice here, and there were animals in Dr. Kaycee's house in big wire boxes and horses out back in the pens. And he already liked the twins.

"Look," Zach said, pointing to a corral nearby. "Claire's giving a riding lesson. Let's go watch."

And maybe they'd let him see his uncle now and then.

• • • •

"HELLO AGAIN."

Cimarron smiled at the sound of Sarah's voice before he turned around. She'd changed into jeans and an aqua sweater that brought out the brilliant blue of her eyes. Her long red hair was caught by a clasp at the nape of her neck, hanging in waves down her back.

"Hello, yourself. No more corporate executive?"

"No. Didn't do me much good, anyway."

The disappointment in her voice rang clear. She probably wasn't having good luck getting her money, based on the way the old house looked right now.

"I'm sorry to hear that. So you're free the rest of the day? What's left of it."

"Yes, I love Mondays. Aaron and I prep as much of Tuesday's food as we can on Sunday after breakfast and he washes and dries all the linens before he leaves. So I usually have Mondays to catch up on paperwork, bill paying, housework..."

"Do you ever take vacation?"

Sarah smiled ruefully and shook her head. "Not in a long time. When Bobby lived with Mom, they took over for me so I could go away for a few days on a skiing trip with...a friend."

"Deputy Whitman?"

Sarah's eyebrows lifted. "Why do you say that?"

"Wild guess from the way he acted the other night. Are you still seeing him?"

"No. We broke up last year." She examined his progress around the room. "Why are you working so hard on this place, when you probably won't finish it?"

"I like to keep busy and this is what I do."

She sat down dejectedly on a windowsill. After a few moments Cimarron sat beside her, their knees almost touching.

"You're having trouble raising the money, aren't you?"

She nodded. "One excuse after another from the banks. But I haven't given up, so don't start celebrating."

"Sarah, I'll probably celebrate more if you find the money. I don't like this situation any more than you do."

She looked at him in surprise. "You're serious, aren't you?"

"I know about dreams that go to hell with the blink of an eye. If I'd known your plans for this house, I would never have bought it." He shook his head slightly. "But I'm afraid Bobby would have sold it to somebody else anyway."

"My dad's trying to make him sell the RV and give me the money from that."

"That's a start. And I assume Jon Rider's going to invest in the house to some degree from all the questions he asked me yesterday."

"Nothing gets by you, does it?"

"Not if I can help it."

She chewed gently on her lower lip and Cimarron could feel his blood rush harder while he fought the urge to take her in his arms and offer some comfort. No way he could afford to get close physically or emotionally, to open himself to the hope of a future that was doomed before it started. She had to solve her problems on her own.

"This bed-and-breakfast has been a dream of mine since Bobby and I inherited the property from our uncle," she said. At least she had to release her lip to talk, but now it was rosy and a little swollen and he wanted to lean forward and take up where she'd left off. "That's what hurts so bad about him selling out. He knew that."

"I overheard a few things the first day in the café. The contractor said something about you inheriting part and Bobby part?"

"Yes, my uncle Eual wanted to be fair. He left me the café because I'd helped him over summers and school holidays. He knew I was more reliable and a harder worker. And I'd promised him I'd help Bobby with the bed-and-breakfast, but Bobby never had a real interest in doing anything that restricted his wanderlust. I convinced him to sell the house to me and I'd pay him back from the profits once I had the place operational. We were supposed to sign an agreement when he came home, but...Well, you know the rest of the story." The disappointment in her voice was wrenching.

"All too well."

She fell silent, studying her hands clasped on her knees. "So what else are you planning to do?"

"Today? I have the rest of the rotted or damaged windowsills to repair and that's about all."

"I can hammer."

"What?"

"I can hammer, if you show me what you want done."

"You're kidding, right?"

"No, I'm not kidding. Actually I can do a lot of handyman work. Comes with the territory when you own a café." She stood and offered him a convincing smile. "I'm a fast learner and I've got all afternoon off."

Sarah looked totally serious, but the skeptic in Cimarron doubted her intentions. He rose, too. "Why?"

"Let's just say I'm trying to minimize my expenses. If I help, you can't charge me as much." She made a pouty face at him and plucked a hammer from his tool belt. "Try me."

Oh, baby, don't tempt me.

Cimarron bit hard on the inside of his cheek to keep those words in. Quickly he turned away. Clearing his throat, he said, "I...uh...let me get a couple of boards from outside. You wait here."

Alone on the porch, Cimarron sucked in a lungful of cool air. What the hell just happened? A little "pitiful me" from her and he wanted to kiss her happy? That wasn't his usual style. That feeling he had when Sarah bit her lip—where did that come from? Scary.

When he regained his composure, he picked up the sawed boards and took them inside. Sarah waited by the window where he'd left off working. He knelt and she did the same, as he showed her how he wanted the board nailed into place. She wasn't kidding—she knew how to hammer. He followed her along the length of the board, using a nail set to countersink the nail heads.

When they finished, Sarah examined their work closely. "Not a bad job. So what next?"

"Do the same with the other windows that are leaking. Tarp the bad spots on the roof. I'd already have that done, but I'm still waiting for the tarps I ordered to come in."

"I don't do roofs," she said.

"No, I would hope not. This one's about thirty feet off the ground at its lowest point."

"I could if I wanted to." The twitch of her lips and the mischievous spark in her eyes could have been mistaken for seduction.

Surely she was not intentionally flirting with him—or was she? Cimarron instinctively drew back. On purpose or not, this woman was trouble.

"I have no doubt you can do whatever you want to do."

"Oh, I meant to mention this earlier," Sarah said. "I still have to pay you back for repairing my griddle last week. You went to a lot of trouble. How much do I owe you?"

"Nothing. I didn't do it for pay."

"But you bought everything, then did the labor. I'd like to compensate you."

Cimarron lifted an eyebrow. Could he choose the compensation? He gave himself a mental face slap.

"It wasn't a problem."

"Well, I want to do something. I have a couple of nice steaks. Why don't you and Wyatt come around this evening and we'll have steaks, baked potatoes and salad. And I have hot dogs or grilled cheese for Wyatt, if he'd rather have that."

Cimarron considered the invitation with measured reserve. Sarah was definitely working a plan, he just wasn't sure what it was yet. "Why are you suddenly being so nice to Wyatt and me?"

She smiled sweetly. "Well, for one thing, I feel sorry for Wyatt." She slipped the hammer back in place, her hand brushing his side long enough to send a strong surge of desire through him. "And for another, I figure I can be nice to anybody for a month."

A muscle in Cimarron's jaw twitched and he smiled. Two could play this game. "Darling, women have fallen in love with me in less than a month."

Her eyes widened, the pupils growing large and dark. "Don't get your hopes up on that."

"It's not my hopes I'm worried about," he said.

She sucked in a quick breath. "Well, don't worry about that, either. Do you want steak or not?"

"Sounds good to me. Guess I'd better go rescue Kaycee from Wyatt. We'll clean up and be over to help with the cooking."

"I'll get things started. See you in a few."

Cimarron blew out a hard breath as he watched Sarah maneuver the slope down to the café. Even from the back she turned him on now. Time to run like a rabbit. Or keep reminding himself that it was only a game—and he could endure anything for a month.

CHAPTER THIRTEEN

CIMARRON PUT away his tools, locked the house and went to fetch Wyatt. He'd been thinking about what Wyatt told Jon Rider about his daddy having a "fatal." Time for another one of those fatherly talks he always seemed to flub. He expected to hear the children playing, but instead he found only the quiet halls of the clinic. Kaycee was cleaning up in the staff's break room.

"Good afternoon. I hear my nephew's been mooching off you," he said.

Smiling, she shook his hand. "Nice to see you again. Wyatt's a darling little boy, no trouble at all. He's out back playing with the twins."

"I appreciate you inviting him over."

"What's one more?" Kaycee said with a genuine laugh.

"I guess so. I'll take him off your hands now."

"He's welcome to come by and play anytime the kids are here."

"Thanks. I know he'll enjoy that."

Cimarron stopped at the corner of the building. The three boys were standing on the fence rails, chattering softly as they watched a woman in the paddock with a horse on a lunge line and a small helmeted girl in the saddle. He waited for a lull in the riding lesson, then approached the fence.

"Hey, boys," he said. "Having fun?"

"Yes, sir," Zach said. "We're watching Claire give a riding lesson."

"Who's Claire?" Cimarron asked.

"Our ranch foreman's daughter. She goes to Montana State and works at the clinic sometimes."

"Oh, I see," Cimarron said.

"Did you come for Wyatt?" Zach asked.

Wyatt looked around at him, the laughter disappearing from his face.

"Yes. Time for him to come home."

Wyatt climbed down slowly. The twins flanked him like body-guards.

"Can I come back sometime?" Wyatt asked.

"Dr. Kaycee said you could come over whenever the twins are here."

"Tomorrow?" Tyler asked.

"We'll see. And maybe you guys can come over and play with Wyatt, too."

"Sure. All the time."

"Good. We'll see you later, then. Come on, Wyatt."

The boy's crestfallen face said he didn't want to leave, but he told the twins goodbye and accompanied Cimarron back to the apartment.

Cimarron took a deep breath. "Wyatt, we're going next door to eat with Sarah in a few minutes, but I think you and I need to talk."

"I didn't do anything," he said.

"I didn't say you did anything. We need to talk about your dad."

"Oh." Wyatt's face puckered into a confused frown. "Is he coming to get me?"

"Sit down."

Obediently, Wyatt climbed into one of the kitchen chairs and waited.

"Do you understand exactly what happened to your daddy?" Cimarron asked.

Wyatt squirmed in his seat. "Just that he got a fatal and is probably in heaven."

"Do you understand what the word *dead* means?"

Wyatt shook his head.

"I didn't think so." Cimarron made a couple of turns around the room, gathering his thoughts. He ran a shaky hand through his hair. "Where did you hear the word *fatal?*"

"I don't know. I just heard somebody say my daddy got a fatal and was gone like that." Wyatt made a show of snapping his fingers.

Cimarron stooped in front of Wyatt. "Look, Wyatt, this is what happened. Your daddy fell from a tall scaffold. That's like a wide shelf we built at the top of the room for the painters to stand on. He hit the floor really hard. It hurt him inside so much that he couldn't get well again."

Wyatt's face paled. "Not ever?"

Cimarron slowly shook his head. "Not ever. He died. That's what being dead is. When you get hurt or sick and you go to sleep and never wake up again."

"And my daddy's dead?"

"Yes."

"But you said he was in someplace called heaven. I thought maybe that was back in Idaho."

"No, as far as I know it's not in Idaho. Heaven is the place where good people go when they die. Most people think it's up above the clouds and stars and all. We can't see it from here, but some people think that those who died are looking down, watching over the ones they loved." At least, Cimarron hoped that was where R.J. was. No telling, with his lifestyle. But let Wyatt believe the best.

Wyatt's eyes filled with tears. "And he's not ever coming back?" he whispered.

"No. But you'll be okay. I promise."

"Are you my daddy now, Unca Cimron?"

Cimarron laid a hand on Wyatt's small knee. "Wyatt, I wouldn't be a very good daddy. That's why I brought up the idea of all those good families out there with mothers and dads that could do so much better than me."

Wyatt sniffed hard, and Cimarron reached over to put a napkin on the table for him. "Blow."

Wyatt obeyed and Cimarron wiped his nose.

"I like Zach and Tyler's family. Can I go there?"

Cimarron's heart ached. Why couldn't he answer yes to any of this child's questions? Having Wyatt adopted was best for the boy, but Cimarron didn't have the words to make him understand that. "They've already got seven kids. I don't think they have room for another one in their house. But there are many, many good families..."

Wyatt turned his head away. "No, I don't want that. I just want my daddy back."

When he couldn't make Wyatt look at him again, Cimarron rose. "Okay, we'll talk about it later. Right now we need to clean up and go to Sarah's."

Wyatt bathed and put on clean clothes and waited at the table for Cimarron to take a quick shower, dry his hair and dress in jeans and deck shoes, with a sweater over his T-shirt. When they joined Sarah on the patio, she was setting the round glass-topped table. She laid napkins, silverware and cutlery in place, adding sour cream and butter for the potatoes, salt and pepper shakers and bowls for salad. The cool evening was perfect for dining alfresco.

"Charcoal, lighter fluid and matches are in the cabinet against the wall," she said. "I'll make a salad and bring out the steaks. If you don't mind I'm going to microwave the potatoes, since there's not enough time to bake them."

"No problem. I do it all the time."

"Wyatt, would you rather have a grilled-cheese sandwich or hot dogs?" Sarah asked. "Or I can share my steak with you. I never eat it all."

"I like steak, I guess," Wyatt said, dragging his backpack across the deck to the patio table. He took out a coloring book and crayons and started coloring.

Sarah gave Cimarron an inquisitive look. "What's wrong with him?" she asked softly. "Did something happen at the clinic?"

"No, nothing like that. I'll tell you later."

"I'll get those potatoes going."

In the kitchen, Sarah quickly put together the salad and nuked the potatoes. She always felt she was cheating when she did that, but there were times when necessity won out. She got two beautifully marbled steaks from the refrigerator and took them out to Cimarron.

He had the fire going, and the tongs were in his hand. When he turned at her approach, Sarah clapped a hand over her mouth trying not to giggle. He'd donned a silly apron patterned with a woman's curvy bikini-clad body that a friend had given her as a joke.

He shot Sarah a broad grin. "Does this make me look fat?"

Wyatt looked up. His eyes widened in surprise. "Unca Cimron, you look funny!"

Try as she would, Sarah couldn't hold in the bubbling laughter that erupted from her throat at the sight of that very male body "dressed" in a bikini.

Cimarron took the platter of steaks before she dropped it.

"What?" he said, faking insult. "You don't like it. I wore it just for you."

"Oh, please, you're killing me." She wrapped her arms around her body. "My sides hurt now."

Wyatt took up her silly giggles.

"You shouldn't leave stuff like this around. It's pretty lethal."

Cimarron primped and fluffed the apron, making Wyatt laugh until he held his sides, too.

Still chuckling, Sarah returned to the kitchen for a bottle of wine and a couple of glasses. Back on the patio, she uncorked the wine and decanted it for a few minutes. "Hope you like shiraz. It's the vintage of the night. I have juice for you, Wyatt."

The meat sizzled as it hit the hot grill. Cimarron closed the cover and took off the silly apron, then eased down into a patio chair, stretching his legs full length and crossing them at the ankles. Taking the wine, he sipped and nodded his approval.

"What are you thinking?" she asked.

He shook his head slightly, pursed his lips and turned his gaze to the darkening valley. "Nothing. Just enjoying the peace. What are you thinking?"

She shrugged. "What a shock this past week has been."

"I guess so. Took me by surprise, too. Your brother obviously has a serious gambling problem."

"That and a lot more. You don't want to hear that sorry story."

"Probably not. I've got a pretty bad opinion of Bobby already."

She took a sip of wine and pondered his words. Bobby gave a lot of people bad opinions with his loose code of ethics. He had disappointed their parents again and again, but like the story of the prodigal son, the family still loved him and hoped he would change.

"Bobby has some emotional problems from childhood. He was a sickly child and our mom was always afraid something was going to happen to him. He ended up spoiled by the time he was toddling, and he really never had to grow up." Sarah took a deep breath and another sip of wine. "So he does these things without thinking about the consequences."

"That's rough. For him, too, I imagine."

"I think so. It kills Mom how he acts, and it makes Dad angry. But nothing we say seems to get through to Bobby." Sarah shivered and straightened her back. "Anyway..."

"Nobody's family's perfect," Cimarron said, going to turn the steaks and then coming back to his seat. "My dad couldn't settle down to responsibility. Like a kid, chasing the rodeo all over. He—" Cimarron's cell phone rang. He pulled it from his pocket, glanced at the screen and silenced it.

"Take that if you want. I'm going in to get the salad and potatoes anyway."

"I'll catch it later," Cimarron said.

Cimarron's demeanor changed with the phone call—as if a door had closed quietly, like someone wanting to hide a secret without attracting attention. He went back to the grill and this time he didn't return until the steaks were done and the salad was served.

Then he forked a steak onto each of two plates and took his place at the table. Sarah sliced off a portion of her steak and cut it into small pieces for Wyatt and shared her salad and baked potato with him.

"Thanks," he said, and dug in without complaint.

For a while, the only sounds were the scraping of knives against china and the song of crickets in the meadow grass. A movement at the edge of the patio caught Sarah's attention. She motioned in that direction and said softly, "Look."

The stray that had eaten Cimarron's lunch peered around the corner of the patio wall.

"It's the dog!" Wyatt cried, jumping up from his chair.

"Sit back down," Cimarron ordered. "I told you to leave that mutt alone."

Disappointed and embarrassed, Wyatt climbed back into the chair and watched the dog intently.

"Go away," Cimarron said with a flick of his hand.

The dog ducked behind the wall out of sight.

"Why are you running her off? She hangs around for scraps now and then."

"That's the dog that stole my food at the river."

"She usually doesn't come this close to the house. Maybe she likes you."

"My lot in life. Dogs like me."

"And that's not good?"

"Just something else to be taken care of. Besides, the sandwiches were in the pocket of my best jacket and she stole that, too."

"Oh, bad dog," she said in a tone of voice that indicated she was more sympathetic to the dog. She began to gather the napkins, plates and utensils on the tray to carry them inside.

Cimarron narrowed his eyes at her. "Real bad dog. I'll clean the grill."

When Sarah returned with a tin plate full of scraps, the stray dog sat a few feet away from Cimarron, her head cocked. He closed the lid on the grill and put everything away. Sarah held back in the doorway watching the man eye the dog and the dog eye the man. Wyatt had edged off his seat and Sarah could see his eagerness to get closer to the dog.

Cimarron shook his head. "Not gonna work, girl. You'd better latch on to somebody else."

The dog whined at the sound of his voice, her tail thumping the stone floor. Even though Sarah often fed the stray out of pity, the animal had never shown the least hint of being friendly.

"Looks like you have a friend, whether you want it or not."

Cimarron's mouth twisted into a grimace. "I don't think so. She'll figure it out."

Sarah approached with the steak and bread bits and set the plate down on the edge of the patio. The dog eyed her warily, then moved toward the food. Sarah stepped back but Wyatt moved forward, squatting close to the dog. Sarah reached out to pull Wyatt farther away. The dog snarled and snapped at her hand. She snatched her hand back, whapping Cimarron squarely across the cheek.

Cimarron jumped between her and the dog, jerking Wyatt away at the same time.

"Back off!" he yelled at the dog.

The dog bolted. Cimarron sat Wyatt in the chair.

"I told you to stay away from that dog."

The child began to sob. "I'm sorry. I'm sorry. I wasn't going to touch it. I just wanted to watch it eat."

"Well, now you know better." He scooped Wyatt up. "You need to be in bed."

Sarah didn't intervene, even though she wanted to take the weeping child in her arms and comfort him, something his uncle obviously wasn't going to do.

To Sarah, Cimarron said, "Thanks for the steak. I'll talk to you later."

"Sure. Good night, Wyatt."

When they were gone, she went inside and cleaned off the counters, put the dishes in the dishwasher and went back outside to sit at the table and have another glass of wine. She felt sorry for Wyatt. Did Cimarron never give him a comforting word? Today in the old house she'd felt an attraction to Cimarron, but now she wasn't sure. Any man who acted so heartlessly toward a child wouldn't fit her bill as a…as anything.

The metal pan scraped across the deck. The scruffy dog was back, gobbling the food, her stance tense, ready to flee at the smallest threat. She looked up at Sarah with a guarded gaze as she licked the last crumb from the pan. Suddenly, she pricked her ears and ran.

Cimarron's footsteps vibrated on the wooden deck.

"I saw you still out here. Sorry about what happened. The dog didn't bite you, did it?"

"No, she didn't bite me."

He sat on the patio chair near hers.

"More wine?" she asked.

"Sure."

She set the full glass on the table near him, then noticed his reddened cheek where she'd accidentally slapped him. "Oh my gosh, I'm so sorry."

Instinctively she reached to touch the red mark. He caught her hand.

"That's what you get for trying to be good to strays."

"She seems so lonely. I hate to turn her away."

"It's your fingers you're risking."

Cimarron's thumb caressed those fingers and their eyes met. Sarah caught her breath and waited. He leaned across the space between them until they were so close their lips almost touched. He tipped his head just slightly, as if testing.

Was she going to sit there and let him kiss her? A complete stranger? An enemy? Suddenly aware of how secluded they were in back of the café, out of sight of the passing cars, she pulled back slightly. He kept his fingers entwined with hers and turned her hand over to plant a kiss in the center of her palm, without taking his eyes from hers.

"You could get yourself in a lot of trouble being so kind to strays, Miss Sarah," he said softly.

She jerked her hand away, flustered. "Did you get Wyatt to sleep?"

Cimarron's hand remained motionless for a moment, as if her hand were still there. Then his fingers curled around his wineglass and he took a sip.

"Finally. I left the light on and the door open and I can see it from here. I don't think he'll be as scared if he wakes in the apartment."

"That's good. It bothered me that he was so frightened the other night."

"I know. You're very good with kids. I noticed how you handled Kaycee's brood."

"I love children. I get the feeling you don't," she said bluntly.

He made a wry face but didn't deny it outright. "I'm not good with them like you are. Don't have a clue what to do with one."

"That's obvious. You hardly say a kind word to Wyatt."

He set down the wineglass with a look of surprise. Surely he realized how he treated the child. But maybe not, because he frowned and shook his head slightly.

"That's not really fair. I'm doing the best I know how. I've just never been around kids. Then all of a sudden, he's dumped on me."

"That's a pretty way to put it."

"It's the way it felt when it happened. I had a bad feeling giving R.J. a job to begin with. Then he brought Wyatt to work that day and expected me to babysit because his girlfriend had run off. It made me furious and I told him to get his work done fast and come back for the kid."

For a long minute, Cimarron stared into the dusky half-light that covered the landscape like a gossamer cloth. A shiver ran down his body. "I think he was rushing to get finished and that's why he fell. He died on the floor before I could tell him...anything."

"I'm sorry. So sorry."

Cimarron pressed his lips together tightly as though sealing in his emotions so that she couldn't see them. Then he shook off the mood and said, "I've figured out already that being sorry doesn't help one bit. If it did, I'd change a lot of things."

"Don't you have family to help out?"

"None. My mother died when I was a teenager. My dad's been absent most of my life and frankly I don't know if he's still alive. Even if he were, I'd never saddle Wyatt with a life like the one I led. He deserves better."

"He'll be all right. He's a very agreeable boy. More than most."

Cimarron grunted. "Too agreeable. I wonder when he's going to blow again like the other night. I was panicking when you came up there."

"He just needs comforting, Cimarron. He's lost his daddy and he's scared. He needs to be hugged and reassured."

"Something I'm not good at. And my lifestyle. How will he adjust to moving every year or so? And who's going to keep him while I work? Day care? Strangers? It's not best for him." He blew out a hard breath. "Anyway, I don't have a clue what to do about Wyatt."

"People have to adapt when the unexpected happens. Maybe you'll need to change the way you work. Find something more stable."

Cimarron clapped his hands on his thighs and rose. "Yeah, exactly. I have to change my way of life, stop doing the only thing I love and know how to do because my brother got himself killed. Just great." He shoved his hands into his jeans pockets and took a deep breath. "Sorry for unloading on you. It's just that...Never mind. I've bothered you too much already. Thanks again for the steak and taking Wyatt over to play. See you."

Cimarron crossed the deck to the apartment and closed the door behind him, shutting out most of the light from inside. Eventually the apartment fell dark. Sarah remained outside until she grew cold from the night air. She cupped to her nose the hand Cimarron had held, inhaling the fading traces of his cologne. The spot he had kissed, dead center of her palm, tingled as if she'd touched a live wire. He was one frustrated man right now, and she had no idea how to help him—or his sad little nephew—any more than she knew how to help herself. She wondered why that mattered to her at all, but it did.

CHAPTER FOURTEEN

GET A ROOM in the motel. This woman will be your undoing.

Cimarron leaned against the closed door of the apartment, staring into space, trying to figure out why he was so hurt by Sarah's censure of him for the way he treated Wyatt. Her disappointment sank into his belly like a lead weight, made his mouth dry, his skin hot, as if he had a fever. He squeezed his eyes shut, to block out the sight of the sleeping child on the low trundle bed.

God help me, I'm doing all I know to do! I don't know how to raise this child.

His instincts told him to run like a scalded dog if Sarah's opinion weighed on him this heavily. Ever wary of losing his independence, he never allowed himself to grow dependent on a woman. Never cared one iota whether they approved of him or what he did. Casual dates. One-night stands. Those he understood.

This time felt different, even though he and Sarah hadn't got off to a great start. Even though she was playing the be-nice game with him. Even if the attraction was one-sided. Cimarron took another shower, this time a cold one, before crawling into bed, wishing he could go back to the day before he hired his brother.

The next morning, Cimarron cooked eggs and biscuits from a can for himself and Wyatt before going to work. The twins were at day camp, so Wyatt had to entertain himself again. He wanted to play outside with his toy cars, and Cimarron agreed but told him to stay on the porch.

Today's jobs involved basic waterproofing, repairs and prep work that all had to be done regardless of who continued with the project. And he had no intention of charging Sarah for any of it. He welcomed the mindless physical work because it kept his mind off his problems temporarily.

Hours later, with one wall primed to repair the aging plaster, hunger pangs finally enticed Cimarron to break for lunch. As he approached the foyer, he heard Wyatt talking softly. Before he reached the doorway, he stopped short. There was Wyatt lying on his stomach with his arm around the stray mutt, talking earnestly to her. Her tail thumped happily on the boards of the porch and she cocked her head to the side as if listening to every word.

Cimarron stifled the urge to run the dog off again. Sarah's criticism still stung, and obviously the dog had had ample opportunity to bite Wyatt before now.

"I wisht you could be my dog," Wyatt said. "But my uncle won't let you."

The dog gave a low whine and licked Wyatt's face. Wyatt giggled, then put his finger to his lips.

"Shh, we don't want Unca Cimron to hear us and get mad. He'll make you go away again. Do you live in the woods? I'd let you sleep with me. Sarah gave us a good room with a soft bed and you could sleep in it, too. If you could stay, I'd have somebody to play with all day."

Cimarron stepped onto the porch. The dog pulled away from Wyatt and slunk down the steps. Wyatt jumped up.

"I didn't go get her," he said, talking fast, his face flushed with anxiety. "I promise, I didn't. She came up here and lay down."

"It's okay, Wyatt. I'm not angry."

"You're not?" Wyatt looked uncertain about that. "I thought you didn't like that dog."

"It's not that I don't like the dog, I was afraid she'd bite you."

Wyatt brightened. "She didn't. She's real friendly."

"I see that."

"Can I keep her, Unca Cimron? Can I?"

"I don't know if that's a good idea…" Cimarron didn't care if the dog hung around, but he was concerned that Wyatt would grow attached to the mutt and have to leave it behind. "See, she still might be sick, even if she's friendly. The only way you can keep her is if we can get Dr. Kaycee to examine her and give her shots for rabies and other diseases."

"Shots?" Wyatt said with a look of disgust. "She won't like that."

"Probably not, but it's the only way. Will she come when you call her?"

"Don't know. Didn't call her." Wyatt sounded as if he suspected his uncle was trying to trick him.

"Well, try. I won't run her off."

Wyatt went to the bottom of the steps and squatted. "Here, girl. Here, girl," he called, clapping his hands and looking around. The dog was nowhere to be seen. "Come on. Nobody's gonna hurt you."

Cimarron hung back and after a few moments, the dog crawled out from under an overgrown shrub at the corner of the house. Warily she approached Wyatt until she saw Cimarron and she stiffened. Cimarron squatted, too, even though he was on the porch, hoping not to intimidate her.

Her matted tail wagged the least bit as she nosed into Wyatt's hand. Wyatt grinned. "She came."

"I see. Let's see if she'll follow you home then, and we'll feed her something. That'll keep her around."

"Oh, boy!"

Wyatt jumped up and the dog backed off a few steps, but when he called her, she followed as he trucked down the hill to the apartment. Cimarron followed a few yards behind. Whenever he approached, the dog bounded away and waited for him to put distance between them. In the apartment he put together a plate of scraps left over from breakfast and added a few slices of sandwich meat.

Outside on the deck, Wyatt wanted to feed the dog, but Cimarron wouldn't let him. "She still might be aggressive about food. Looks like she hasn't eaten in a while. You stand aside and we'll see how she acts."

The dog could smell the food. She licked her chops and braved Cimarron's presence to inch closer. Friendly as she was to Wyatt, he figured she must have had a home at one time, so he tried a basic command to see if she'd been trained at all.

"Sit."

The dog eyed him hard, then considered the dish in his hand. She plopped down on her haunches.

Cimarron gave Wyatt a wink. "They'll do anything for food."

He put the dish on the deck and stepped back beside Wyatt. "Okay," he said.

The dog swished her tail from side to side, still wary, but hunger soon got the best of her and she sidled up to the dish. She bolted the food in three bites and looked to Cimarron for more.

"She'll eat us out of house and home," he told Wyatt. "Go get the rest of the sandwich meat."

Wyatt ran inside and returned with the package of ham. Cimarron made the dog sit while he retrieved the dish and filled it with food. "Now you put the dish down a few feet away from her and come back here."

Wyatt did as he was told. The dog could hardly sit still, but Cimarron reinforced the command and she stayed.

"Now," he said quietly to Wyatt. "You tell her okay."

"Okay, girl. Okay."

Eagerly the dog rushed to the dish and made quick work of the meat, again looking to Cimarron for more, but this time with a toothy dog grin on her face. "Guess we'll have to get her some real dog food, if she's going to eat like this. *If* we can get her shots, understand? And at first you're not to feed her unless I'm around."

"Can we name her?"

"I guess so. Any suggestions?"

"Spot."

"She doesn't have any spots. How about Splinter. She's kinda like a splinter. She's brown like a splinter and she gets under your skin and you can't ignore her."

"Splinner. I like that name. Come here, Splinner."

Having licked the plate clean, she trotted to Wyatt's side.

"Will you ask Dr. Kaycee about the shots today?" Wyatt asked, fondling the dog's ears.

"After work. And the sooner I get back to it, the sooner I get through." He made a peanut butter and jelly sandwich for Wyatt and one for himself, then poured a couple of glasses of milk.

Today he wanted to finish prepping the walls in the parlor. Tomorrow he planned to have a good look at the roof, to see what needed to be done there. He'd found water damage during his inspection of the attic and he needed to find the sources of the leaks and at least get a tarp over them before the next heavy rain.

After they ate, he worked another couple of hours in the parlor, periodically checking on Wyatt and Splinter as they played together outside. That dog might be a good thing, after all, he thought, going back inside to finish up for the day.

"Hey, Sarah," Wyatt called.

"Hey yourself, Wyatt. What have you got there?"

"That dog. Unca Cimron says we might keep her, if she's not sick and Dr. Kaycee can give her shots."

"Really? I hope you can."

"Me, too. I love her. We named her Splinner."

"Is your uncle inside?"

"Right here," Cimarron said from the doorway as Wyatt nodded. "What can I do for you?"

"I've got a couple of hours free. I thought maybe I might help again."

"If I'd known that, I would have worked slower," Cimarron said, wishing now that he had. "I've just finished."

"Look, Unca Cimron! Zach and Tyler are home," Wyatt shrieked. Wyatt waved wildly to the twins and they saw him and waved back, motioning for him to come over. "Can I go play?"

"You can't go over there every afternoon. They have other things to do than play every day, I imagine. You need to wait until you're invited."

Wyatt looked as if he'd been deflated. "Dr. Kaycee said I could come anytime."

"I know, but you need to be sure they don't have other plans. Just be patient. I'm going to clean up in here and we'll go over and ask Dr. Kaycee about the dog."

Wyatt blew out a frustrated breath and sat down hard on the top step, with his chin in his hands, watching his friends go inside the clinic. The dog laid her head on his lap and he absentmindedly stroked her ears.

"You want to come in and keep me company while I put everything away?" Cimarron asked Sarah.

"Sure, why not," she said without smiling.

He'd gotten on her bad side again about Wyatt, he guessed. No way he'd ever measure up to her standards. So why let it worry him? But he cringed every time she gave him that disapproving look.

"So you're keeping the dog?" she said, once they were out of earshot of Wyatt. She went around the room, picking up his tools and handing them to him to put away.

"I got reamed out last night for being so mean. I figured I better toe the line and be nice to the kid."

"I didn't ream you out. Just gave you some friendly advice."

"Well, I took it."

"Last night you thought the dog might be vicious. What changed your mind?"

"I went outside and Wyatt had his arm around her. At that point, I figured the horse was out of the barn. Keeping her is still conditional. If we can't catch her for an examination and shots, she's not hanging around here."

"What'll you do, shoot her?" That disapproval in her voice again.

"No, I'm not going to shoot her. Just keep her run off."

"Let's hope she's okay, then."

"Yep." Cimarron put the last tool in the tool chest and wiped his hands on a towel looped through the handle. "Well, let's see if she's going to cooperate."

The dog followed Wyatt to the clinic.

"I'll get Kaycee for you," Sarah said. A few moments later the two women emerged from the clinic.

"So she finally came to somebody, did she?" Kaycee said. "I've been trying to catch her for months."

"Her name's Splinner," Wyatt said proudly.

"Good name," Kaycee said. "I'd like to get a blood sample, too, to see if she's got heartworm or other problems. Come help me prepare everything, Sarah. She might do better if we're not around."

As soon as the women were out of sight, Cimarron took Wyatt into the corral.

"Call her in here."

Wyatt called and clucked to the dog. She slowly approached but hesitated at the gate, as if sensing a trap. Wyatt called again and she came inside. While Wyatt held her attention, Cimarron quietly moved around to close the gate. Then he stooped beside Wyatt and held out his hand until the dog sniffed it and seemed to relax.

Just wait, Cimarron thought. *You'll never trust me again.* Cimarron dreaded what he had to do, but it was for her good, so he spoke reassuringly and she allowed him to pat her. He tested the waters by draping his arm over her back. She jumped but didn't try to get away.

"Good girl," Wyatt said. "You're a good girl, Splinner."

"Now look, Splinter," Cimarron said. "You're not going to like this, but you've got to trust me, okay? I wouldn't let anybody hurt you. Well, no more than a shot, anyway. Wyatt, when Dr. Kaycee comes back, I want you to go inside and play with the twins, okay? I'll call you when we're done."

"But, Unca Cimron—"

"She might try to bite. Do what I say, or we'll have to let her go."

"Okay," Wyatt said with a scowl.

Kaycee came out of the clinic and Cimarron explained the agreement he'd made with Wyatt. Kaycee sent him in through the back door, where Sarah waited just inside. When the door closed, Kaycee put her equipment down nearby.

"Hey, Splinter," Kaycee said with a gentle but firm voice. "This won't take but a minute of your time. Have you got her, Cimarron?"

"I hope so."

He tightened his hold just slightly and felt her tense. He began talking, keeping his voice even as she strained her head around. Kaycee knelt on the other side of the dog. Splinter lifted her lips in a low snarl.

"It's okay, girl," Cimarron soothed, expecting to feel sharp teeth sink into his arm any minute. "Be still. That's a good girl."

In a few quick, quiet movements, Kaycee swiped the dog's skin with antiseptic, popped the shot and rubbed the spot to get Splinter's attention off the sting. So far, so good. Although she was stiff and still growling deep in her chest, she hadn't tried to bite.

"I'm going to attempt to get a little blood, but I'll need you to hold her leg. Are you game?"

"Yep, let's do it. Tell me when you're ready."

Kaycee quickly arranged her instruments on a towel that she laid on the ground beside Splinter. Cimarron rubbed the dog's chest and touched her leg to see how she reacted. Her frightened eyes turned his way, and deep inside he saw trust that he hadn't expected—that might not be there in another couple of minutes.

"Okay," Kaycee said.

Cimarron took a firm grip on Splinter's leg with one hand as he kept her confined with an arm around her body. Kaycee was good, really good. She ran the needle under the skin and bright blood filled the syringe. Splinter yelped and struggled, but Cimarron held on until

Kaycee withdrew the needle. By then the dog was frantic and no amount of talking was going to calm her down. Kaycee swiped the needle site with another antiseptic swab.

"Let her go," she said.

Splinter tore out of Cimarron's loosened grip and headed for the gate, running up and down the fence until Cimarron got there and swung the gate open. She streaked away and disappeared into the woods on the other side of the old house.

"So much for Wyatt's dog," Cimarron said. "Probably for the best anyway."

"She'll be back. She's scared, but she likes you."

"Not anymore."

"Wait and see." Kaycee gathered her things.

"Thanks for taking care of her. You're good with that needle."

"Well, thank you. Come inside and get her tags. When she comes back you can put a collar on her and keep animal control at bay."

"If..."

Inside, Cimarron bought a red collar. Sarah leaned on the counter watching. "So you got it done?"

"She didn't act up nearly as much as I expected," Kaycee said. "Cimarron kept her calm."

Funny, he doesn't have that effect on me, Sarah thought, idly playing with a pen on the counter as Cimarron attached the tags to the collar ring with a pair of needle-nose pliers Kaycee handed him. "So, where is she?"

"Hightailed it for the woods as soon as she got loose," Cimarron said. "Like I figured she would." He handed the pliers back and jingled the tags playfully. "Probably wasted money on this collar. And now I've got to tell Wyatt."

"Let him stay here," Kaycee said. "I'll have Claire feed the boys after they play a little longer. Maybe the dog will be back by then."

Cimarron seemed tense and out of spirits as he and Sarah strolled around the café to the back deck.

"A glass of wine to unwind?" Sarah offered.

"Why not." He tossed the collar onto the patio table and slumped into a chair, laying his head back, staring at the scudding clouds overhead.

She brought the bottle and a couple of glasses and asked Cimarron to pour.

"Worried about the dog?" she asked,

He shrugged. "More about how Wyatt's going to take it. I hated to see her frightened. But she'll be better off with the shots. Maybe keep her from getting sick."

"You like that dog, admit it."

He nodded slightly. "I guess. Wyatt sure does."

They sat in silence as the sun dropped low over the mountains and cool shadows crept across the slope behind the old mansion.

"Something else is bothering you," she ventured.

"I've been thinking about what you said last night. About the kind of attention Wyatt needs."

"And?"

He tilted his head and looked over at her. "I think you're right—and I can't give it to him."

"I didn't say that. I just said he needs more love and understanding right now."

Cimarron sat up in the chair, leaning his elbows on his knees, holding his wineglass with both hands. "I know, but I've never been that type of person. I'm not sure I can change who I am."

"You've been thrown into a difficult situation. It's going to take time for things to settle down, become normal again."

"That'll never happen. I wouldn't know normal if it slapped me."

"You told me you didn't have family—that's got to be tough. I've got parents who would do just about anything for Bobby and me."

"Lucky," Cimarron said. "My old man wouldn't give me the time of day. Even before my mom got sick, he was on the road following the rodeo most of the year. After she began to get worse—part of which was because of him being gone and us having no money—he basically deserted us." Cimarron shook his head. "It was rough."

"What about Wyatt's father?"

"There was always that 'dad likes me best' thing. Dad liked him best because he learned to ride broncs before I was old enough, and he took off with dad when I was around eleven or twelve."

"With your mom sick? They left you there alone with her?" Sarah asked, unable to comprehend a parent who would do that.

"Yep, like broncs busting out of the chute. Both of them were so glad to escape, the door never hit their butts on the way out."

She couldn't imagine a twelve-year-old with such responsibility. She'd thought babysitting Bobby was tough when she was twelve...

"Am I being too nosy if I ask what was wrong with your mother?"

"She had serious heart problems. I don't really know what all. We didn't have money for doctors and sometimes not even for her medicine. She was too proud for welfare and got what money she could from taking in ironing when she was feeling all right. She didn't want to burden me with her condition, but I knew it was bad from the time I was young."

Bitterness seeped into Cimarron's voice. Sarah saw a different man than the one she'd thought she knew. Vulnerable, the lingering fear of desertion almost palpable.

"By the time I was a teenager, I was afraid to leave her alone for long. I went to school and worked part-time in the afternoons. That was about it. I wanted to quit school and work full-time so she could get treatment, but she got so upset whenever I mentioned that I just gave up and we did the best we could. All she wanted was for me to finish high school."

"So did you?"

"Oh, yeah, I finished." Cimarron swirled the wine in his glass, staring into its depths. The way he said it...the brittle emotional edge to his voice, made her more curious, but she waited for him to go on. Finally, he set the glass on the table. "She died the night I graduated."

No wonder he had trouble coping. Just imagining her mother gone turned Sarah icy with dread. Even now that she was grown. She couldn't fathom losing her mom as a teenager.

"Oh, Cimarron, no."

"What's worse is that I wasn't there. A girl I liked threw a graduation party and invited me. Usually I would have stayed home, but Mom insisted I go and have a good time. And I did—until I got home. She'd had a massive heart attack and died. The doctors told me there wasn't anything I could have done—" His voice broke and he closed his eyes. "But at least I could have been there."

She laid a hand on his arm. "Don't be so tough on yourself. You had no way of knowing."

"But I should have. The excitement of the night. Seeing at least one of her sons graduate. The exertion of walking the distance from the parking lot to the gym. All that strained her heart. I should have known."

He put his head in his hands, staring at the cracks in the deck.

"She had such a hard life. It would have been nice if she'd lived long enough so that I could have provided for her. Today, I could give her just about anything she wanted, a nice house, medical care. But back then all I could do was be there for her—and I wasn't, when she needed me most."

"But you can't change that. You can't go back. If you don't forgive yourself and go on, it will eat away at you forever."

"Don't I know that."

After a few minutes of silence, he rose and stretched with an easy grace, muscles bunching, his abs outlined by his knit shirt. So much pent-up anger and resentment, so much apprehension about raising his nephew. Yet she sensed a survivor instinct in him and she felt sure he would find his way in time.

The more she watched him work on the old house, saw his attention to detail, the pride he took in his work and in even the most menial of repairs, the more she wished they had a different relationship. She wanted her house back, but she also wanted Cimarron to restore it. She knew it was a futile dream and she had no idea how to make it happen, but she wanted it anyway.

He gave a crooked, boyish grin when he caught her watching him. "Let me help you clean up before Wyatt gets here." He picked up his wineglass and the bottle and went into the café with Sarah behind him.

· · · ·

Cimarron washed their glasses, set them upside down on the draining rack and leaned against the counter, drying his hands on a paper towel as he studied her face. She attracted him in a way no other woman had. Something about her scared him and excited him at the same time. She made him want to come clean and confess his sins; made him want to escape the fortress he'd built around himself to stay safe from the world. Or at least let her inside with him. Treacherous life-ruining thoughts that could destroy all he knew and understood. Thoughts that pressed against his better judgment until he knew he should run. But his boots might as well have been nailed to her floor, because he couldn't take a step to save himself.

"Let's see, you serve great wine, make the best coffee and milk shakes I've ever had. You're an excellent chef and a passable amateur shrink. You're beautiful and industrious and smart. Anything you don't do well?"

Sarah bit her lower lip, a habit that Cimarron found charming.

"Wow. Such flattery. I wouldn't want to reveal my weaknesses. Maybe you'll just have to find out for yourself."

That was an idea that had already crossed his mind. Cimarron couldn't resist that rosy lip anymore. If she slapped him silly, he'd know better next time. Certainly would be fun to build something with her, and he wasn't thinking about the house.

He straightened and moved closer, gauging her willingness. Tonight she didn't evade him but stood her ground as if waiting to see what he'd do. He leaned down to brush her lips with his. She lifted her face toward him ever so slightly, putting that rosy bottom lip within reach. Delighting in her sweetness, he nibbled the coveted lip for a moment, then, when she still didn't resist, he covered her mouth with his.

For a moment, she didn't respond, but then she put her hands on his shoulders and drew him closer. He deepened the kiss and pulled her against his body, every muscle taut with anticipation, his heart thudding harder with every flick of her tongue against his.

He curled his fingers into her thick, shining hair, pressing her lips harder to his, losing himself in the warmth of her mouth, relishing the soft caress of her hands along the sides of his face.

"Cimarron, stop," she said suddenly, struggling to get out of his grip. But he wasn't ready to let go. She pushed at his shoulders until he backed off a few inches. "Somebody's coming," she whispered urgently.

Then he heard the voices outside, moving closer.

"Sarah, are you around?" Kaycee called.

Wyatt! He'd forgotten about Wyatt. Again.

"Sarah?" Kaycee called from the deck. "Have you seen Cimarron? I've brought Wyatt back."

"In here," Sarah said, her voice hoarse and flustered.

Cimarron caught her arm. Before she could pull away, he pushed a lock of damp hair off her cheek and tucked it behind her ear. He said softly, "Fix your hair a little."

"Thanks," she whispered, fluffing her hair into place as she hurried through the door, calling to Kaycee. "We're in here. Coming."

Cimarron followed. Wyatt caught Sarah's hand.

"Sorry, I'm so late getting him back. I had some paperwork to finish."

"No problem," Cimarron said. "I know he enjoyed it."

Kaycee leveled an undisguised look of appraisal on both Sarah and Cimarron. Why did he feel like shriveling under her scrutiny like a kid caught with his hands in the cookie jar? One glance at the beard burn on Sarah's delicate skin answered that. They were caught red-handed and red-cheeked, and from Kaycee's look she didn't necessarily approve.

"Well, I'd better get going. Long drive home," Kaycee said.

"Thanks again," Cimarron said.

When Kaycee left, Cimarron said, "Sorry. I think I got you in trouble."

"She's a friend, not my keeper," Sarah said, raising her gaze to his. "But we need to talk later."

Talk, talk, talk. The last thing he wanted to do with Sarah was talk. But Wyatt looked exhausted and, now that he'd cooled off somewhat, Cimarron wasn't sure if he could afford to get emotionally involved with her.

Yeah, like it's not already too late for that.

"Where's Splinner?" Wyatt said, looking around frantically for the dog.

"She kind of ran off after the shot. Scared her a little."

"Will she come back?" Wyatt cried.

"Guess we'll have to wait and see," Cimarron said.

"But I want her real bad," the child wailed.

I know the feeling.

"Nothing we can do about it tonight. Let's go. I think we both could use a shower."

CHAPTER FIFTEEN

THE NEXT DAY, Cimarron made four trips up the tall ladder to move supplies to the steep roof. Several tarps, which had finally been delivered, one-by-three strips of wood, screws, cordless screwdriver, safety harness and ropes.

He'd been working about an hour when he heard a dog bark. The dog barked again. Splinter. So she'd come back. But she was making a terrible racket.

"Wyatt?" He'd left his nephew playing outside the door of the apartment. Ordinarily, Wyatt obeyed well, but a rise of panic caught Cimarron when he glanced down and realized the child was not in sight.

"Wyatt, answer me!" he yelled, playing out the rope attached to his safety harness so he could reach the ladder against the side of the house.

"I'm here," Wyatt called back.

When he couldn't locate the boy's whereabouts, he said, "Where?"

"On the ladder."

No way! A cold sweat broke out on Cimarron's body as a small curly head popped above the roofline. Thirty feet up.

"Wyatt, stay right there. Don't move!"

"I'm okay."

"*Don't...move!* I'm coming for you."

"I want to come up there with you."

"Damn it," Cimarron muttered. "Wyatt, stay where you are."

Cimarron scrambled toward the edge of the roof. His boot hit a patch of debris. He lost his footing and began to slide, catching a glimpse of Wyatt trying to step onto the roof. Grasping for a hold on the rope, Cimarron scraped his boots across the uneven shingles, cracking them, sending shards pattering over the edge of the roof. Well, he might not have to worry about Wyatt or anything else in a few seconds.

He slid toward the brink with terrifying velocity. Heart hammering, grappling for any handhold, he prayed his safety rope would hold when he hit the end—and that Wyatt didn't fall off the ladder in the meantime.

• • • •

Sarah came out the back door of the café to toss a bag of trash. She looked toward the house, where she knew Cimarron was working. Squinting, she tried to make out what the blob was at the top of the ladder.

"Oh my God...Wyatt!"

She broke into a run, sprinting as hard as she could. Then she saw Cimarron moving down the roof. He lost his footing, began to slide. Sarah thought her lungs might burst as she plowed up the hillside and caught the sides of the ladder. Wyatt teetered at the very top, one foot on the roof already.

"Wyatt! Don't go on the roof. Don't."

Thank goodness the ladder was securely tied off and didn't sway much as she climbed. Debris showered down on her. She could hear Cimarron scrambling to stop his fall, but she couldn't see him from her vantage point. Only the small boy, his face contorted with fear.

"Unca Cimron! Don't fall!"

Rung by rung, Sarah pulled herself up. Never mind that she hated heights. She forced herself to concentrate on the top of the ladder, and not think about how far it was to the ground.

"I'm scared!" Wyatt wailed, looking down at her.

"I'm coming. Hang on. Don't let go!"

She thought it must be a good sign that Cimarron hadn't plummeted past her yet.

After what seemed to be hours she neared the top. Four rungs left to reach Wyatt's foot. Just then, Cimarron reached over the edge of the roof and caught Wyatt's arm.

Sarah made the last few rungs, placing shaky arms on either side of Wyatt and hanging on for dear life.

Wiping his sweating brow on his sleeve as he hung on to his rope with one gloved hand and Wyatt's upper arm with the other, Cimarron said in a hoarse voice, "Can you get him down?"

"I guess I have to," she snapped. "What were you thinking, letting him on this ladder."

"I didn't let him. He...We'll talk about it on the ground, okay? Just help him down."

She glared up at him and said through gritted teeth, "I *hate* high places."

Slowly, slowly, she backed down the ladder, having to steady herself at the same time she helped Wyatt's short legs make the long gaps between rungs.

When they were at a safe distance below, Cimarron swung onto the ladder and followed them down.

She knelt and took Wyatt into her arms, hugging him tightly. "Are you all right?"

He nodded, face pale but otherwise unharmed.

"Run down to the apartment and wash your hands, okay?" she said. "We'll be right there."

Wyatt ran off with Splinter at his heels. Sarah turned her wrath on Cimarron as he stepped onto the ground.

"How did he get on that ladder? He could very well have been killed."

"I know that," Cimarron said, his voice still raspy as he tried to catch his breath. "I was trying to get to him."

"Yes, and you almost got yourself killed in the process."

"He wasn't supposed to be up there. I told him to stay close to the apartment."

"You told him? Don't you know anything about young children? They don't—"

"No, and hell no! I don't know a damn thing about raising kids. I told you that."

"Then you'd better learn quick."

"Why don't you just tell me how to raise him, since you know so much. Save me the time and effort."

"I know enough to realize he needs supervision if he's running around here playing."

"Won't be a problem much longer," he said abruptly.

"What do you mean by that?"

"Never mind. I'm taking care of it." He brushed past her and strode down the hill and into the apartment, slamming the screen door behind him.

Sarah's heart thumped hard against her ribs, even though Cimarron and Wyatt were both unharmed. She wasn't sure which had scared her more, Cimarron sliding toward the edge of the roof or the little boy in danger of toppling off the ladder.

She did know, however, that a young child was in need of supervision and she couldn't ignore that. She walked directly to the clinic to talk to Kaycee before she started dinner prep.

"Hey," she said, knocking on Kaycee's office door. "Busy?"

"Nothing that can't wait. Sit down." Kaycee put down her pen. "You're white as a sheep. What's wrong?"

"Cimarron and Wyatt. They're going to give me a heart attack."

"What happened now?"

Sarah described the incident on the roof.

"That's not good. Both of them could have been hurt."

"Or worse," Sarah said.

Kaycee leaned back in her desk chair. "We can't let that go on. He needs some help."

"He needs a lot of help. I've never seen anybody as clueless about kids as he is."

"Maybe he's never been around children."

"That's what he says, but you'd think there'd be some natural fathering instinct in there somewhere."

"He's not Wyatt's father, remember. And he'll find those instincts in time."

"Where?" Right now, Sarah wasn't in the mood to admit he had any good qualities.

"Sarah, the man's trying. Even I can see that. The way he handled the dog situation. I don't think he wanted that dog but Wyatt did, so he made sure it was vetted first. He could have just run it off."

"I guess so. But he can't keep working in that house with Wyatt running around unsupervised. Even if I wanted, I couldn't help much because of the café."

"I agree with that."

Sarah gazed out the window to the holding pens in the back of the clinic. Claire walked beside a small helmeted girl on a horse. She spent most of her days at the clinic, when she wasn't in class at MSU in Bozeman.

"I was thinking maybe Claire might be willing to babysit for him sometimes. Times when he needs to do something dangerous like climb around on a thirty-foot-high roof."

"She'd probably like that. She's trying to save all she can to start a therapeutic-riding school when she graduates. She's here all day three days a week, and she studies or helps me out most of the time when she doesn't have riding lessons to give."

"Would you ask her for me? I have to get to work. I'm behind already."

"I will, as soon as she finishes her lesson."

"Thanks. Guess I'd better be going."

"Sarah, don't give up on Cimarron just yet. I got the feeling last night you were warming up to him. He'll figure out how to be a father yet, if you help him a bit."

• • • •

C IMARRON SENT SARAH a dozen roses for helping him out with a sitter for Wyatt three days a week. She didn't mention the roof incident again, but her opinion of him as a father was clear. He agreed with her fully and hoped his lawyer would find an adoptive family soon. Parting with Wyatt was going to be hard enough under any circumstances, but Cimarron was growing more attached to him with each passing day. Something he had never intended to do. Feeling that bond tightening around his heart scared him as much as his growing attraction for Sarah did.

Then he had to deal with the house. The way things were going he needed to get away fast, before this constant craving for Sarah got out of hand. That put him in a quandary. If she couldn't come up with the money, he would have to hang around long enough to get the house ready to sell—out from under her again. He'd gotten a lot more work done today without Wyatt underfoot, but he was far from ready to put a For Sale sign out front.

Damn it, why didn't things ever work out?

Cimarron had showered and started a load of clothes washing in the apartment's stacked washer/dryer combo by the time Claire brought Wyatt home. Wyatt's face broke into a wide smile reminiscent of R.J.'s happy-go-lucky spirit as Cimarron caught him up and hoisted him overhead.

"Hey, buddy, how'd your day go?"

"Great!" Wyatt said, giggling with delight as Cimarron kept him suspended and jiggled him back and forth. "I got to play with Zach and Tyler."

"What did you play?"

"Lots of stuff. Cars and cowboys, and Claire played games with us."

"What a day. Wish I'd been there instead of in that stuffy old house."

Cimarron set him on his feet again.

"You come with me next time."

"Maybe I will. Run inside and wash your hands and I'll make dinner in a minute."

He turned his attention to Claire, pulling out his wallet. "I can't tell you how much I appreciate this."

"He's no trouble at all." Clear hazel eyes and a friendly smile made Claire pretty, even without the benefit of makeup. Her straight brown hair was pulled on top of her head in a ponytail and she spoke in a no-nonsense manner that Cimarron figured kids and horses probably obeyed without question. "Such a sweet little boy."

"He is, isn't he." He pulled fifty dollars from the wallet and handed the money to her.

"Oh, Mr. Cole, that's way too much. I keep the twins when they're here, anyway, and one more's no problem."

"Call me Cimarron. And it's not too much for the load you took off my mind, believe me."

"Thank you. Um, I was wondering if you've thought about putting him in day camp with the twins, then he could go to kindergarten in the fall and make some friends."

A pang of guilt gnawed at Cimarron. "I'll think about it, but I'm not sure we're going to be here long enough for that. I'd hate to get him started and have to pull him out."

"Oh, okay. I thought maybe you were fixing up the old house to live there. Don't know where I got that idea."

"Probably not. Anyway, I'll pay you daily, if that's okay with you."

"That's fine. I'll be at the clinic day after tomorrow around eight. Bring him over anytime after that."

"Thanks again."

Inside, Wyatt had his toys out and sat on the floor at the foot of the bed, entertaining himself, as he did much of the time, as if trying not to bring attention to his presence.

"How does a toasted cheese sandwich sound?" Cimarron asked.

"Okay."

Another obvious lesson gleaned from the life he'd led—Wyatt ate anything that was put in front of him. He didn't complain about anything. He didn't talk back. Shy and quiet, he was too good, in Cimarron's mind. Little boys were supposed to be mischievous, daredevil...loud.

"You want to help?"

"Sure. But I don't know how."

"I'll show you. Come on."

Cimarron set a chair backward against the small cabinet near the stove. Wyatt climbed up, which put his head about shoulder level with Cimarron.

"You butter the bread. Like this." Cimarron spread a layer of soft butter on the bread and handed Wyatt the butter knife. The child's expression was a mixture of pride and worry. He took the knife and dipped it into the butter, wobbling the tub. Cimarron steadied it before it turned over and was rewarded by Wyatt's grateful look. Concentrating mightily, with the tip of his tongue sticking out the corner of his mouth, Wyatt held the bread and spread the butter in an uneven swath, then glanced up at Cimarron.

"Nice job for your first try."

Wyatt beamed. "I'll do the rest."

"Good." Cimarron sliced the cheese into thin rectangles. He put half the bread, buttered side down, in a large frying pan. "Now put the cheese on the bread. And be careful not to burn your hand."

When Wyatt did that, Cimarron had him put the other slices of bread on top. He browned the sandwiches on both sides until the cheese oozed out, then transferred them to plates, which he set on the table. "Can you get the milk from the refrigerator?"

"Okay." It was a gallon jug, but half-empty, and Wyatt managed to haul it to the table. Cimarron poured full glasses and let Wyatt put the milk away while he sliced an apple and divided the wedges between the plates.

"Mmm, good," Wyatt said, chewing his first bite of cheese sandwich.

"Must be the way you buttered the bread. That makes a difference."

Wyatt's face lit with pride. "Thanks."

They ate in silence for a few minutes, then Wyatt said, "Zach and Tyler's first mom died, like my daddy did. They said they knew how bad I felt about it. They said their mom's in heaven with my dad." Wyatt continued to eat without showing much emotion, though Cimarron could sense the conflict the boy must be feeling. "I don't think about it if I can help it. Zach said they did the same thing. And it's a lot better now that Dr. Kaycee's their second mom."

"I'll bet that's true. Dr. Kaycee's a nice lady."

"She sure is. I wish I had a mom like her."

"I wish you did, too, Wyatt. I really do."

"I wish I knew where my mom is. She might be looking for me."

Cimarron put his sandwich down, his appetite gone. How did he tell this child that his mother wanted to forget that he'd ever existed? If Cimarron admitted he'd called her, would the truth break his nephew's heart? If he didn't, would Wyatt always hold out hope of her finding him and taking him home? This daddy business had not been in his future plans. How the hell did he get here? And how did he get out?

"Wyatt," Cimarron said, careful in choosing his words, "did your daddy tell you anything about your mother?"

A look of profound sadness crept over Wyatt's face and his shoulders slumped as if the weight of the world had dropped on him. "My daddy said she was a bad woman. Real bad. And she ran out on us and wasn't ever coming back. He said she didn't never love me from the start and was mean to me."

Whoa! Good job, R.J. Kill the kid with the truth, why don't you?

"What do you think about that, Wyatt?"

"I wish she wasn't bad. Zach says all moms love their kids, but my daddy said my mom don't and I wish she did."

The boy looked at Cimarron with such confused longing in his eyes that Cimarron had to bite back a curse. R.J. had snatched away Wyatt's innocence long before he died and left him alone in the world.

Exhaling slowly, he gathered his wits and searched for the words this little boy needed to hear. "Wyatt, I didn't know your mother at all. But I heard your daddy talk about her some. And I think he was probably pretty angry with her when they parted, and that's why he told you those things. If you want my two cents' worth, I think your mother did love you in her own way. But from what your daddy told me after you were born, she was way too young to be a good mother because she was still just a teenager herself."

Wyatt squirmed in his seat, but his intent gaze never left Cimarron's face. When Cimarron hesitated, Wyatt said, "What else, Unca Cimron?"

Cimarron cleared his throat and continued. "See, she neglected you right after you were born—that means she didn't feed you right or keep you clean like she should have. So your daddy was afraid you might be hurt, and he had a judge give him full custody of you when you were just a baby. But that meant that your mother had to give up all her rights to see you."

Cimarron forced a small white lie so that Wyatt wouldn't keep expecting his mother to find him, or maybe want to go looking for her. "So she really can't take you back now. And she won't be looking for you because she knows she's not supposed to see you."

Wyatt blinked rapidly, holding back the tears that threatened to overflow. "Never?"

Cimarron pressed his lips together tightly and shook his head. "I don't think so." Why did life have to be so hard? "But, look, buddy, you're going to be okay. I'm going to make sure of that. So don't worry about your mom anymore, deal?"

Like switching television channels, Wyatt diverted his attention to something else. "Are you going to read to me tonight?"

"Sure. What do you want to hear?"

When they'd gone shopping, in addition to toys, Cimarron had bought a stack of books. He'd been appalled when the child didn't recognize any of the most popular children's stories. Cimarron bought favorites that his own mother had read to him, as well as any books with covers that interested Wyatt. Now they had a nightly ritual. Supper, Wyatt's bath, Wyatt tucked into his trundle bed, and then Cimarron lay on the big bed beside him and read until the child fell asleep.

While Wyatt bathed, Cimarron cleaned the kitchen and turned down the bed. His cell phone rang and he answered. On the other end, his lawyer greeted him.

"I think I've found the perfect couple to adopt your nephew."

Cimarron's stony silence prompted the lawyer to ask, "Are you there? Did we drop the connection?"

"No, I'm here," Cimarron managed to say. He'd been dreading this call more than he realized.

"You heard me? I've found an excellent family for Wyatt."

"Yes, I heard. I...I don't know exactly what to tell you."

"They would like to meet with you next week to discuss the arrangements. They have impeccable credentials and can take him almost immediately."

"Immediately? Look, I'm not sure now that I want to have my nephew adopted. I need more time to think about it."

"I see. I wish you'd told me before I contacted these people. We've all gone to a good bit of trouble to help you out."

"I understand. I should have talked to you about this sooner." Cimarron leaned against the door frame, staring at the old house on the hill, afraid to make this decision on the spot.

"Might I suggest, Cimarron, that you come to the meeting next week and talk to the Carringtons. I know you were concerned about trying to raise the boy alone. These people have two children of their own and three they've adopted. I believe you'll find they are an ideal family for Wyatt."

"When next week?"

"Tuesday...2:00 p.m. Will you be there?"

"All right. I'll come. But I'm not committing to anything, at this point."

"I assure you, you won't find a better placement."

"Thank you for your effort."

Cimarron clicked the phone off as Wyatt ran from the bathroom in his pajamas, flew across the room and leaped onto the bed. He hadn't thought about the bathroom door being ajar, but apparently Wyatt hadn't overheard him. Cimarron held the covers and Wyatt scooted underneath.

"Let's start with this ABC book about animals, and then I'll read you a story."

Cimarron had also found that Wyatt didn't know his ABCs or how to count to a hundred when he'd first arrived. Now he could, and he was quickly learning to read simple words. The ABC book had colorful illustrations and Cimarron often caught Wyatt looking at it on his own, repeating the words he'd been taught. Claire was right. He needed to be in a learning atmosphere.

Cimarron hung over the edge of his bed so Wyatt could see the book, and they progressed through several pages. One of the pictures showed a bear hibernating, with z's coming from his mouth. Wyatt wanted to know about the z's.

"That means he's snoring when he sleeps. Like this," Cimarron snorted a little and Wyatt fell into a fit of giggles.

"You make funny noises when you sleep, Unca Cimron."

"I do? How do you know that? You're supposed to be asleep."

"Sometimes I'm awake. And I hear you."

"Well, all real men snore."

"They do?" Wyatt pursed his lips and pointed to the next page. "What's that word?"

"Camel."

They progressed all the way to H. Wyatt yawned a couple of times. Cimarron put the book aside and picked up *Grandfather Twilight,* one of his favorites. He began to read. After a few pages, he grinned. Wyatt's eyes were closed tight and his ribs rose and fell as he emitted a series of noises that could have passed for snoring. Cimarron read on, and before long the boy slept soundly—and quietly. Cimarron closed the book and stared at the peaceful face. He gently brushed back the curly hair, wondering what he should do with this child who had wormed his way into his uncle's heart.

CHAPTER SIXTEEN

THE SOFT SCENT of roses filled Sarah's bedroom as she dressed for work. When she passed, she put her nose among the twelve perfect blossoms in shades of palest blush to deep, vibrant pink and inhaled the sweetness. Ordinarily flowers this beautiful would have had Sarah's spirits singing, but this morning they had only increased her conflicted feelings toward Cimarron.

Her future was up in the air because of him, and she was no longer sure what she wanted to do about it. Her quest for money had fallen far short of the sum she needed, yet she no longer stayed on the phone every spare moment, trying to scrape up more. She hadn't resigned herself to failure yet, but she was considering a different strategy.

Little Wyatt had grown on her. Such a sweet child in need of security and reassurance. She knew Cimarron loved him. Yet he couldn't show it, and Wyatt was the loser.

She'd grown accustomed to Wyatt's giggles and to Cimarron's killer grin, which never failed to make her heart skip a few beats, and she sometimes saw glimpses of that inner man he so closely guarded. His fear of responsibility and commitment had deep roots, but Sarah held out hope that if he stayed long enough they might get to know one another better, become friends—or maybe something more, something much more.

She put her fingers to her lips, remembering the way he'd kissed her. She could almost feel his touch, feel the trembling inside that waited, breathless, for more. Did she dare dream of having her house back and gaining a family in the deal? Not yet, so she tucked that dream into a safe place and went downstairs to work, hoping he'd show up. If not, she'd pop over to the house during her break. She enjoyed working side by side with him, learning from him, picking up on his philosophy of preserving history by restoring priceless old buildings.

Only, that posed a worse dilemma than before. At the end of the month, unless a miracle happened and money floated down from heaven, she would have to admit defeat. She wanted her house back, but she felt it should be restored correctly. And Harry Upshaw wasn't the man to do that. Cimarron was. Yet she couldn't afford Cimarron's fees. The thought of the house languishing, dark and empty, made her cold inside. She warmed immediately, however, when Cimarron walked through the door and shot her a grin that would have melted butter.

• • • •

E VEN THOUGH HE'D FED Wyatt before sending him off with Claire for the day, Cimarron had decided to have breakfast in the café. The hunger inside him had nothing to do with eggs and biscuits, however, and he was gratified that Sarah seemed really glad to see him.

After he ate, he hung around until the other customers left. Aaron cleared the tables and took piles of dirty dishes to the kitchen. Sarah wiped the counter in front of Cimarron.

"Claire took Wyatt today?"

"For the whole day. Are you coming to help later?"

"I planned to. Is that okay?"

"More than okay," he said, laying down the money for his breakfast. "I'll be waiting."

He had finished tarping the roof, with Wyatt safely in Claire's care, and had begun a preliminary Internet search for replacement tiles that would match the original ones. Now that moisture was no longer a threat, he could begin repairing the damage inside the house.

Outside, sawing a section of molding to size, he saw Kaycee Rider arrive at the clinic and returned her wave. He'd been impressed by the ideal family she and Jon had created. For the briefest moment, he pondered the possibility of raising Wyatt himself—if he had Sarah to help him. An image formed in his mind of him and Sarah, married, living in the big old house, with maybe another child or two to keep Wyatt company.

An unrealistic bubble of a dream. Sarah had no interest in him, other than being nice for a month to get her house back. On the other hand, it seemed as if she was being more than nice when he'd kissed her the other night. The flush on her skin, the eager look in her eyes, the lips uplifted to be kissed again. *Much* more than nice, in his estimation.

"What are we working on today?" Sarah jolted him from his daydream.

"This parlor. I've replaced most of the damaged wood, so hopefully the remaining holes and cracks can be filled with compound and sanded."

Once Cimarron had showed her what to do they worked for almost two hours without a break and with little conversation, but it didn't seem to matter. He felt comfortable in her presence, with no pressure to keep up idle chitchat. The quiet room was peaceful and he breathed in the scent of raw wood, acrid wood putty and the rich fragrance of the outdoors drifting through the open windows.

A light blue baseball cap covered most of Sarah's bright hair and she wore a tight T-shirt and jeans that made concentrating almost impossible.

Finally he gave up. "Let's call it a day."

"Good idea. I have to get back to work before long."

She sat on the windowsill while he capped containers and cleaned putty knives.

"Does Wyatt like staying with Claire?"

"He loves it. Thanks for setting that up."

"You're welcome. I was really afraid he might get hurt."

"I know. I guess I figured he'd always do what I said." Cimarron put away the tools and held out a hand to help her up and pull her close to him. "Listen, thanks for all the help you've given me with him."

"You're getting the hang of it."

"I don't know, Sarah. I wonder if I'll ever be good for him. Sometimes I think..." Cimarron hesitated. "I think he'd be better off..."

He felt guilty that he was considering putting Wyatt up for adoption, even though he felt Wyatt would benefit in the long run. He really wanted to talk to somebody who would give him an objective opinion.

Sarah put her hands on either side of his face, looking earnestly into his eyes. "He's fine, Cimarron. Everything's going to be all right, you'll see."

She pulled his face down and kissed him, tentatively at first. Then her soft mouth parted, her tongue playing along his teeth enticing him to let her in. The woman had no idea what she was starting. A man had only so much self-control and being near Sarah every day lately had eroded most of his. Her baseball cap fell off and a cascade of fiery hair tumbled around her shoulders.

He drew back slightly, fighting the urge to lay Sarah down right there and learn everything there was to know about her. She moved with him, making a soft, throaty sound. Never mind self-control. Cimarron pulled her tighter into his arms, his hands spread across her back. He kissed her this time, deeply, strongly—searching, finding, taking.

• • • •

By the time he lifted his lips from hers, Sarah was breathless. Desire turned his eyes black as onyx and he, too, drew a ragged breath. Did she want this? She sensed that if she struggled, he would relent. She didn't move.

He smelled good, even after working all day, a trace of aftershave lingering on his skin, with the slightest whiff of male musk that aroused her most primal instincts. Giving way to impulse, Sarah wrapped her arms around his neck. Her fingers played in the soft, dark curls along his nape and Cimarron's low moan triggered a spike of satisfaction that made her raise her lips to be kissed again. He pressed himself against her as his lips covered her mouth, letting her know beyond doubt that she'd thoroughly aroused him.

He was downright beautiful for a man, rock hard everywhere, and he had a kiss that could trigger a meltdown. Maybe she needed to give more credence to her brother's judgment. Her insides sizzling and her lips tingling for more, she reached under his shirt and ran her hands up the firm, hot skin of his abdomen and chest.

He caught her wrists and stopped her, pulling back.

"Are you sure you want to go there?" he asked, his voice husky and strained. "Because you're driving me insane as it is, and I don't know if I'd want to stop if..."

Did she want to stop? She pulled her hands away as she probed deep into his eyes, looking for an answer. He was breathing short and fast, almost panting, waiting for her response. She knew she had only to say the word and the passion that made him quiver beneath her touch would be released and take her places she'd never been. Places that would change everything about her life forever.

She so wanted to feel that. She wanted this man to take her there. But she wasn't sure she was ready and Cimarron must have sensed her reluctance. He stepped back, turned away and put his hands behind his head, staring at the ceiling, regaining control.

"Sorry," he said, when his breathing had returned to normal, and he faced her again. "I shouldn't have..."

Flustered and uncertain what to say, she nodded slightly. "It's okay. I'd better go back to work...now..." She backed out of the parlor, then fled to the café.

· · · ·

AFTER A GRUELING dinner shift Aaron and Sarah finished the cleanup and prep for the following morning, and then Aaron left through the back door. Sarah loaded the night's linens into the large washer and started a wash cycle. When she turned back to the kitchen, she jumped, startled to find she wasn't alone. Deputy Griff Whitman stood in the doorway. He took off his hat, curling the brim in his hands as he moved closer to her. "Hello, Sarah. Guess I missed dinner hour. Had a call out on the highway."

"You haven't been around in a while," she said, wishing he hadn't turned up tonight.

"Haven't had much time. Do you have a sandwich or something for a starving man?"

"Sure."

Though she was dead tired, she made Griff's favorite roast beef sandwich and a cup of coffee from instant powder and water heated in a teakettle. He sat at the prep table to eat.

"What brings you by tonight?"

"Been missing you, one thing."

Not something she especially wanted to hear right now. Griff took big bites of the sandwich, washing them down with hot coffee. "This is good. I've sure missed your sandwiches."

"Come in any time. But try to make it when the café's open," she said lightly.

"Yeah, I know it's late. You look beat. I won't stay long—unless you ask me."

Griff shot her a wink and a grin. When he got no response from her, he grunted and turned his attention to the sandwich.

Between bites, he said, "I don't mean to get in your business, Sarah, but I heard about your problem. Trying to raise money to buy your house back."

"Well, I guess life throws curveballs sometimes, huh?"

She hated her business being talked around town, but she'd been so desperate for money she'd asked just about everybody.

"Ticks me off, that SOB buying your house and asking such a high price for you to get it back."

Sarah made a fresh cup of coffee for him. She didn't really want to discuss the house with him. He'd never wanted her to buy it from Bobby, so why would he care?

"Is he still living in his truck?"

"No, he's renting the apartment."

"What? Now, Sarah, you don't want to let him get a—"

"Don't start, Griff. That controlling attitude's why we couldn't make a go of it. If it was just him I probably wouldn't have offered, but he's got that little boy."

"You and that soft heart for kids."

He finished his sandwich and stood to face her, his expression serious. "Why didn't you come to me when you needed money?"

"Griff..."

"No, really, you know I could help you out."

Griff worked for the sheriff's office because he loved the work. But he had plenty of money through an inheritance from his grandfather that he'd invested well. Never a spendthrift, he had built up quite a fortune. He had been the first person she'd considered—and then crossed off her list. She did not want to be indebted to Griff unless she had to be. At this late date, however, several hundred thousand dollars short of Cimarron's asking price, that might be the only way she could afford the house.

"I heard he was asking well over a million for that dump."

"It's not a dump. It's going to be beautiful when it's finished."

"So, are you not going to get it back?"

"I want to, but..."

"But what? I'm standing here telling you, I'll give you the money to buy it."

"Griff, it would take me forever to pay you back. I don't know that I'd even be able to afford the renovations after I bought it."

He snaked his fingers through his thick blond hair and his blue eyes took on a look of longing that used to lead to something more than handholding. His clean-cut looks and tall, lean frame tended to quicken the local girls' hearts, and the uniform didn't hurt. He was a good dancer and he loved to hit the dance halls every weekend.

"I...I always held out hope we might get back together," he said. "I'll help you build whatever you want."

Where did that come from after all this time?

"And break hearts all over Little Lobo? You don't want that."

"Oh, come on, darlin'. You know I didn't pay any attention to all those girls."

"I remember very well."

Back then, Sarah hadn't missed the surreptitious looks and outright flirting from other women. Griff ate it all up, yet he tended to become aggressive if another man so much as looked at her. Afterward, he'd sulk for days until she cajoled him into a better mood and swore she didn't care a thing about anybody else.

"You never wanted me to run the café. And you hated the idea of a bed-and-breakfast. That was another reason we broke up."

"I know, but I've had a lot of time to think, and I know how much your independence means to you. I'm fine with it now."

Things certainly could turn around in a heartbeat. Except she didn't believe a word of his miraculous change of heart.

"I don't know what to say, Griff. It's a generous offer, but I doubt our relationship would work any better the second time around. We're just so..."

"Think about it. Don't make a rush decision. And if you want the money for the house, you've got it. No strings attached. I've got a lot more than I know what to do with, and Bobby never should have sold that house to a stranger. Call it justice but take the money to get your house back."

"It would have to be a loan, with interest. I wouldn't have it any other way."

"I'm good with that. Let me know."

"Okay. Thanks," she said sincerely. "I'll run some numbers and see where I stand."

"Just give me a call when you make up your mind. Good night, Sarah."

Sarah locked the door after Griff left, and then went upstairs, still stunned by his offer. She could have her house. If Griff said no strings, he meant it. But what if she regained her house—and lost Cimarron and Wyatt?

CHAPTER SEVENTEEN

LIFE HAD MADE such an about-face all of a sudden that Cimarron was afraid to wake up each morning for fear he might be dreaming. He waited impatiently every day of the following week for Sarah to join him to work on the house. On the days when Wyatt wasn't around, they acted like teenagers in love, teasing, playing and getting to know one another more than making any significant progress on the house. When she wasn't there Cimarron worked like a man possessed, in order to keep his thoughts off her.

Impossible hopes and dreams ran through his mind. Suppose he kept Wyatt, and suppose Sarah loved him, and suppose they tried to make a family...When he got to that point in his thinking, overwhelming doubt shut him down. What if he couldn't be all they needed him to be? What if he failed them, too, as he had his mother and R.J. What if, what if, what if? There were moments when Cimarron wanted to squeeze every thought out of his head.

By the time Sunday came around, Cimarron needed a break. When Sarah closed the café after breakfast, he was waiting in the kitchen, helping Aaron finish early so the young man could go home.

"What's on the agenda today?" Sarah asked, sounding eager to get to work as always.

"Nothing."

"Nothing?"

"I'm just flat tired. And you have to be, too. Everybody needs a day off and today's supposed to be warm and sunny. Let's pack a picnic lunch and escape."

Her blue eyes sparkled with anticipation. "Okay. Where?"

"I haven't been fishing in three weeks."

"Oh." Not so much enthusiasm now.

"What?"

She shrugged. "I don't fish very well. Bobby and Daddy always made fun of me, so I quit trying."

"Wyatt doesn't either, so don't worry about it."

Sarah laughed, filling Cimarron with pleasure and making him half wish Wyatt wasn't coming along. But Claire wouldn't be at the clinic today, and he wanted to make up to the child the for previous time, when he'd lost his temper.

From a cabinet, Sarah pulled out a picnic basket straight from a Norman Rockwell painting, complete with plates, cups and utensils, all strapped into place, and a tablecloth folded under the lid.

"You're prepared for any occasion, aren't you?"

"It's what I'm good at."

"Oh, I'd say you're good at a lot of things." He grinned and she blushed. *Perfect.*

He helped her pack fruit punch and soft drinks. Peanut butter and jelly sandwiches were tucked beside ham and turkey subs. Grapes, apples and brownies completed the basket. Then Cimarron went to his truck for fishing gear and a thick blanket.

"Come on, Wyatt. Let's go," he called. Wyatt jumped off the edge of the deck followed by Splinter, who had benefited from a good bath and grooming. "Let's go."

Cimarron carried the basket and Sarah brought the blanket and the fishing tackle. As they went along, Wyatt threw a plastic toy now and then for Splinter to chase. Boy and dog raced ahead on the shady path as Cimarron and Sarah followed at a more leisurely pace.

Impulsively, Cimarron hooked an arm around her neck and pulled her closer. "I'm glad you came. I've been missing you."

"You just saw me yesterday."

"Still missed you."

When they reached a flat clearing near the broad stream, Sarah spread the blanket and sat down.

"Oh, no, no sitting," Cimarron said, assembling a fly rod.

"I told you I don't fish."

"*Didn't* fish. I'm going to teach you the right way."

"You'll end up laughing at me, too."

He leaned over and bussed her cheek. "Only in a good way.

"Look, Wyatt, I think this rod will do for you," he said, pulling a lighter rod from the case.

Wyatt gaped, his gaze fixed on Cimarron's fingers working deftly to fit the joints of the rod together, attach the reel and feed the line through the eyes. He took the rod from Cimarron as if it were gold in his hands. Cimarron snipped the barbed hook out of a small fly and tied it on the end of the leader.

"That's yours now. I want you to take care of it."

"Wow," Wyatt breathed. "Mine?"

"Ready to try them out?"

Cimarron worked with Wyatt first, showing him how to hold the rod. He tucked the end of the rod into the child's long-sleeved knit shirt and led him through a couple of casts, then stepped back to let the boy try for himself.

Cimarron's deep laughter and Wyatt's giggles filled the air as Wyatt slung the line again and again into the swift stream, having too much fun to worry about catching fish. Sarah raised her face to the sun, enjoying the warmth, drifting pleasantly on her thoughts.

"Your turn now," Cimarron said, pulling her out of her reverie and to her feet.

Fly-fishing lessons gave Cimarron an abundance of excuses to put his arms around her to teach her to cast, or to catch her hand and guide it into the correct form. Her reward for small successes was a kiss, and her eagerness to learn increased with each touch of his lips. Before the lesson was done, kisses replaced casting two to one and the fly line lay ignored across the surface of the water.

Sunlight danced on their faces. A dragonfly lit on Sarah's baseball cap, then flitted away. She shifted closer in Cimarron's arms, her back pressing against his chest as he nuzzled her neck, sending goose bumps along her skin.

"Unca Cimron, my line's stuck in the bush."

"Fishing lesson's over," Cimarron whispered in her ear, giving it a gentle nibble that sent tendrils of pleasure curling through her. "Let me untangle him before he gets frustrated."

"I'll get the food ready."

Sarah shook out and smoothed a checkered tablecloth in the center of the blanket and arranged the spread.

Nearby, Wyatt and Splinter rolled and tussled and chased one another amid playful shrieks and benign growls while Cimarron put Wyatt's rod in order. On his way to the picnic blanket, Cimarron caught Wyatt and swung the laughing child over his head.

"Ready to eat?"

"Food!" Wyatt yelled. "I'm hungry!"

"Me, too." Cimarron set him down and Sarah patted the blanket. "Come sit by me, Wyatt."

She parceled out sandwiches, drinks and chips, and the three of them joked and ate. Like a family. Like they were meant to be? More and more, Sarah hoped so.

"Miss Sarah, you make the best food. Even your PBJs are good."

"Thank you. That's the best compliment I've ever had."

After they ate, Wyatt frolicked with Splinter on the riverbank while Sarah and Cimarron cleared the remains of lunch, then relaxed on the blanket, making small talk. Cimarron stretched out, braced on one elbow, and Sarah sat cross-legged, fashioning leaf jewelry like she had as a child. She'd give Wyatt a necklace before they left. She glanced up at the small being who had so suddenly become a part of her life. So much a part of her life that when he wasn't around the world seemed chilly and far too quiet.

"Wyatt, don't throw the dog toy so close to the water," she called.

Too late. Plop! The lightweight plastic bone landed a foot from shore and was quickly caught up by the current. Splinter splashed into the water after it.

"Here, Splinner. Here, girl. I'll get it!" Wyatt called, scrambling onto an overhanging rock to reach out for the toy that was bobbing on the current inches away. The dog trotted back to shore.

"Cimarron, go get him. He might fall in," she said, pushing up from the ground.

Wyatt retrieved the toy as it swept close to the rock. Then he lost his balance, teetering on the uneven footing.

Sarah broke for the riverbank a step behind Cimarron. He hoisted himself onto the rock in one athletic motion—just as Wyatt plunged over the edge with a loud yelp. Cimarron jumped down after him.

"Wyatt! Cimarron!" Sarah cried as they disappeared from sight.

She raced to the jutting rock and clambered up. The stream was shallow at that point, but swift and strewn with rocks. Farther down, the swirling water plummeted over a steep cascade into a deep pool. Cimarron waded toward Wyatt who flailed at the water as the current tugged him downstream.

"Come get me, Unca Cimron!"

"You're okay, buddy," he said. "I'm coming."

"Cimarron, get to him. Hurry!" Sarah cried from the rock.

"Calm down, Sarah. You're making things worse," Cimarron called to her.

Worse? Worse! The child might drown and Cimarron was making precious little effort to save him. How was she making that worse?

She jumped down from the rock and waded in, too. A wild splashing nearby startled her. Splinter bounded past her into the stream, tongue lolling, wanting to play. Cimarron pushed hard through the shin-deep water, closing the gap until he could touch Wyatt.

Instead of grabbing him, Cimarron said, "Come on. You can make it by yourself."

"I can't!" Wyatt shrieked, slapping the water frantically. "I can't swim!"

Cimarron laughed and Sarah fumed.

"Grab him, Cimarron. He said he can't swim. Help him!"

She wasn't making good headway across the swift current, but her fear drove her harder toward the floundering child. Cimarron had maneuvered himself downstream of Wyatt, but still he didn't touch him.

"You don't have to swim. You're sitting on your butt and your head's above water, buddy. Just stand up."

Wyatt stopped fighting and looked at the water swirling around his waist.

"Oh," he said.

Splinter bounced to his side, licking his face, making him smile. He caught a handful of the dog's rough coat and pulled himself to his feet.

"Why didn't you pick him up?" Sarah demanded, grabbing Cimarron by the sleeve. "He could have drowned."

Cimarron gave her one of those get-up-and-walk-it-off looks, engineered to separate tough guys from overreacting females. "I wouldn't let that happen," he said. "But Wyatt needs to learn how to get out of trouble when he gets into it. Look at him—he's fine."

Wyatt had the dog around the neck, trying to dunk her, but Splinter was having none of it. She edged toward shore with Wyatt hanging on, laughing.

"I don't care. He could have been hurt. You should have...done...oooh...*something!*"

"You're worse off than Wyatt," Cimarron said with a grin. "Lighten up."

He shoveled a double handful of frigid water at her.

Clenching her teeth to keep them from chattering, she swiped an armload of water back on him, drenching him.

"I hate when you're right." She dodged more water.

Wyatt and Splinter galumphed across the shallow stream to join in the play. Shivering and laughing, they splashed each other until they could no longer bear the cold.

Sarah ran from the stream first and turned back as Cimarron swept Wyatt onto his shoulders.. Water cascaded off Cimarron's chiseled face, leaving a bronze sheen in the slanting rays of the sun. Motionless, she watched him make his way to shore, pushing wet ringlets of black hair off his face and she trembled—but the frigid water soaking her clothes wasn't the only reason for the goose bumps that suddenly prickled her skin.

Amazing how that hard male body could quiver at her touch, yet Cimarron seemed to be waiting for her to give the signal that would take their relationship to the next level. Once upon a time she had thought she was in love with another man, but now she knew she'd been mistaken. A look from Cimarron made her sweat and shiver at the same time. Wanting Cimarron became a constant in her life, filling every empty place within her, creeping into her thoughts when she was supposed to be concentrating on other things. Spinning fantasies in her mind that she had no reason to believe would come true.

Did he know she was falling in love with him? Could he love her? He hadn't put it in words, and neither had she, but his touch, the softness in his eye when he looked at her, the little things he did for her every day told her that he might. Grinning happily, he plopped a dripping Wyatt on the ground next to Splinter and joined Sarah on the now-damp quilt.

"No fish going to be caught in that stream today. We made a good mess of it."

"I don't care." She squeezed the water from her hair, twisting it to wring out all the moisture she could. "It's beautiful out here, isn't it?"

Cimarron eyed her head to toe.

"Certainly is."

"You're so bad," she said with a laugh. "Are you trying to seduce me?"

"Oh, yeah," he said softly. "If we were alone."

· · · ·

She lay back, hands behind her head, and stared at patches of endless blue sky visible through the leafy canopy overhead. Cimarron played with her hair, swirling circles with it, pulling a strand straight and letting go, watching it fall back into its natural curl.

Felt good, her satiny hair trailing across his fingers. The whole day felt good and he was glad they'd taken the time off.

He stretched his arm out, rested his head on it and closed his eyes. After a while, he said, "I knew I had a treasure in that old house. But I had no idea I'd find you here, too."

"Is that a good thing?"

"Oh, yeah."

"For me, too," she admitted. "Even though I didn't think so in the beginning."

"And what changed your mind? Good looks, good kisses—or good taste in women?"

"Getting a lot of free work done on my bed-and-breakfast."

He growled deep in his throat and rose up to hover over her, watching his reflection dance in her eyes. "I like a woman who can be bought."

"I don't come cheap." She traced the curve of his lower lip, shooting barbs of lust through him.

He kissed the tip of her finger. "What's your price...Ooph!"

The breath went out of him as Wyatt and Splinter landed on his back. He braced quickly to keep from collapsing onto Sarah, then rolled on his side and pulled Wyatt between them.

"What you trying to do, break my back?" he said, giving the kid a tickle.

"I'm cold," Wyatt said.

"I guess you are," Sarah said. "We're all still damp. Maybe we need to start home."

"Party pooper," Cimarron said, but he rose and helped her up, then wrapped Wyatt in the blanket for the trek back.

Once there, Sarah suggested, "Let's change into dry clothes, then meet in the café for hot chocolate to warm our insides."

"Good idea."

"Look, Unca Cimron," Wyatt cried. "The twins are at the clinic. Can I go play?"

"Call and see if it's okay, will you, Sarah?" Cimarron said.

Sarah shook her head and smiled. "You're going to have to lighten up on that. Kaycee said he was welcome anytime they were there."

"I'm going to blame it on you if she sends him home," Cimarron said.

"I'll take the flak. He needs dry clothes, though."

"You heard her. Go change, first."

Wyatt raced into the apartment and was back out in minutes with dry jeans and a superhero T-shirt on backward.

"Wyatt, turn that shirt around," Cimarron yelled as he flashed by.

Without breaking stride, Wyatt tugged the shirt up around his neck and back down the right way. The twins ran to meet him and the three boys disappeared around the corner of the clinic.

"You sure it's all right to just let him go that way?"

"In this case, yes. Kaycee's so laid-back with all those kids, and she loves Wyatt."

"It works for me," he said. "Because I get you alone for a few minutes."

"Umm," she said, touching her lips to his. "That sounds promising, but I have to get out of these damp clothes."

"I'm all for that," he said with a grin. "I can help."

She slapped him on the chest. "Bad boy."

He arched an eyebrow. "That's me. Wanna see."

"Meet you back here in ten."

Cimarron showered quickly and dressed in a sweatshirt and jeans. Even so, Sarah beat him to the café.

Bundled into a long beige sweater and brown warm-up pants, she had a pan of milk warming on the stove. "How about that hot chocolate?"

"Mmm, sounds good."

A few minutes later, she set the cups of steaming chocolate on the prep table and they pulled their stools close together.

"I enjoyed today," she said. "Except for Wyatt falling in the water."

"That's what boys do. Frankly I'm glad to see him getting a little more reckless. I was worried about him at first, he was so meek and timid."

"He's getting to know you, becoming comfortable. Before long he'll be testing the limits. Then you'll wish he'd stayed meek and mild."

"Probably. If that ever comes..."

"What do you mean by that?"

Cimarron wanted to talk to her about the adoption. Gauge her reaction to see if he should press on or maybe try to make it as Wyatt's guardian. His decision might depend on her answer.

"See, Sarah, I...When I first got him...Well, I didn't—"

"Unca Cimron! Unca Cimron!" Wyatt burst through the back door, breathless.

"Hey, buddy, something wrong?"

"Dr. Kaycee said ask could I go home with her and spend the night. Can I? *Pleaasee!*"

"I don't know about that..." Cimarron began. But then he considered what a night alone with Sarah might be like. "Did Dr. Kaycee invite you or did you invite yourself?"

"The twins invited him," Kaycee said from the open doorway. "And I agreed. Claire will bring him back in the morning. I think he'd enjoy it."

"I'm sure he would," Cimarron said, getting off the stool to help Wyatt pack a bag. "So what does he need to bring?"

"Toothbrush and PJ's. He's the same size as the twins and we can improvise if we need to. How about it?"

Cimarron smiled. "Why not? Sounds like fun to me."

"Yehaw!" Wyatt yelled, bolting out the door. "Zach. Tyler. I can go!" More *yehaws* joined the chorus and all three boys disappeared into the apartment.

Within minutes Wyatt's backpack was stuffed with his favorite toys and books and a scant few clothes—underwear, a clean shirt, pajamas and a toothbrush. The boys rushed across the yard to Kaycee's waiting Suburban.

"Thanks," Kaycee said. "I'll take good care of him."

"I know you will. And, Kaycee, thank you for being so kind to him."

"Not a problem at all. You guys have a nice night."

Did he imagine that Kaycee gave Sarah a subtle wink before leaving them alone?

"Is this a conspiracy?" Cimarron asked, easing the door closed. Not that he minded if it was. "Are you sure I'll be safe here alone with you?"

She chuckled and gave him an appraising once-over from head to toe.

"Not a chance," she said.

Hot damn!

He locked the door and turned to embrace her. "So what now?"

Her closeness sent tremors of anticipation through him. He'd been crazy to be alone with her for days now. Where the night would end, he had no idea, but Sarah was taking the lead, and he was certainly happy to follow.

Her hands slipped under his shirt, caressing, exploring. He jerked in a gulp of air as she drew her fingernails up his belly and chest. Pulling her tight against him, he tangled one hand in her long, thick hair and tilted her head back, feathering kisses along the curve of her chin and down her throat.

Her slender body arched toward him and she whispered his name. He caught the bottom of her sweatshirt to slip it off, then suddenly jerked away and backed off, struggling to regain control of himself.

"What?" she murmured, reaching for him.

"We don't need to do this," he said, trying to block out the alluring beauty of the woman before him. The one woman in the world he wanted. The one woman he couldn't take like this.

"Why?" she said. "I thought...the past few days."

He took her in his arms, squeezing her tight, determined not to do something wrong, even though it felt so right. "Because I don't have protection and we don't know what the future holds." He certainly didn't intend to follow in his brother's footsteps with the baby-making.

"Not anywhere?" she said, her voice ragged with longing. "Protection?"

He drew back and looked at her. There was no mistaking the flush of passion and desire on her face.

"Haven't needed any lately," he said hoarsely.

"Me, either," she said softly, the disappointment in her eyes gratifying. She stood motionless in his arms for a long minute then she sighed hard and said, "So what do we do for the rest of the night."

Reluctant to release her and feel the cold seep in where her warm body touched his, he closed his eyes and rested his chin on the top of her head. He did not want to give her up for the one night they could be alone together. Surely there was something they could do rather than...what he really wanted to do. "You decide. It's too late to work on the house."

"I know," she said with a hint of dejection that Cimarron felt himself. She leaned back and looked around as if trying to find some diversion. Her gaze rested on the kitchen table where his laptop sat. She pulled away and a smile brightened her face. "I have an idea that might work."

"What?"

"Maybe we actually can work on the house—on the computer! I was impressed with your design for the parlor. I would love to help plan the other rooms."

"Settled, then. We'll put our minds on the computer and not each other," he said, then grinned, "for the most part."

Cimarron brewed coffee and Sarah ran next door to the café and brought back roast beef sandwiches, chips, and pastries to munch on. They settled at the table with their plates and coffee.

"Could we get any closer?" Sarah asked with a chuckle as Cimarron slid his chair against hers.

"I could try." He bumped the chairs together. "We both have to be able to see the screen."

"True," she said.

Cimarron opened the laptop and brought up the design program.

"Let's start with the parlor that you've already started. I have some questions."

Between bites of food, sips of coffee, and frequent kisses, they worked. Cimarron incorporated some of her suggestions and explained why others wouldn't work well. For the most part, she agreed, but told him she was going to reserve her final judgement until later.

Cimarron didn't care. Considering the circumstances, he was happy just to be in her presence, though such close proximity took a toll on his willpower and he could not resist a stolen kiss now and then. She never resisted, instead leaning against him and lifting her lips to meet his. The hours passed as they worked on the upstairs bedrooms and bathrooms. At some point Cimarron brewed a second pot of coffee and Sarah wrapped up in a blanket.

Before dawn, kissing and caressing took the place of work. They wandered outside and sat on the top step of the porch to gaze at the moon. Sarah shared the blanket and he wrapped his arm around her and drew her to his body to ward off the night's chill.

"Thanks, Cimarron," Sarah said softly.

"For what?"

"For a very nice night together without expecting anything...you know." She breathed in the subtle nuances of his breath, his skin, his hair, memorizing them for the times when she wouldn't be in his arms.

• • • •

Cimarron grunted. "Well, it wasn't easy, I can tell you that. You are hard to resist. There were moments when you didn't know what jeopardy you were in. I...uh, I've never been in a situation exactly like this before." He planted a light kiss on her forehead, the tip of her nose, brushed her lips playfully with his.

"Oh sure, Cimarron. Have you never looked at your gorgeous self in a mirror? And you're successful and rich as the devil, to boot. You must have women coming out of the woodwork."

"No pun intended, right?"

She giggled. "Pun intended. Am I right?"

He twitched a shoulder. "I can usually find a date, if I really want one."

"Like I said, you've known all kinds of women."

He leaned back to prop on one elbow, looking up at her with a crooked smile. "But I didn't feel this way about any of them. Ever." The smile faded just a bit. "Never expected to."

"Why?" She eased down lengthwise beside him on the porch, wondering about the shadow that crossed his face.

He fell into deep thought for a long time. "I just never did. I didn't want to get trapped in a relationship. No ties, no responsibilities. Nobody to hold me accountable for anything."

Though Sarah sensed he wanted to say something else, he didn't, so she said, "And now you feel differently?"

"Maybe. In some ways I don't have a choice with Wyatt in the picture. At least not at the moment." He held her gaze for a moment then looked away. "Then there's the house...and you. I don't want to see you hurt."

"I've been thinking about the house, Cimarron. I think you're right."

"Usually am."

Sarah narrowed her eyes at him. "Oh, ho, don't get smart."

"Sorry, go on."

"I mean, it needs to be restored, not remodeled like I had planned."

"True." Cimarron leaned his head on his hand, listening with interest. "So, you have the money to buy it and restore it?"

"I feel sure I can get the money to buy it. Enough to restore it might be a problem." How much should she tell him? As much as she wanted to, she couldn't just write off Griff's offer of a loan unless she could be certain of Cimarron's intentions.

He pulled a thoughtful face. "Well, maybe we can work something out."

Her heart did a double thud, but she worked to keep her voice calm and businesslike—well, as businesslike as one could be lying on the floor beside one heck of a sexy guy, indirectly talking about a future together. At least she was.

"I was hoping so. You're the only one I'd want to do the work."

"Me, too."

"How can we manage it?" she asked eagerly.

He opened his mouth to answer when Sarah's cell phone buzzed.

Darn it! Sarah answered to hear Kaycee's voice.

"I tried Cimarron's phone but didn't get an answer. Just a heads-up in case you two are *dishabille*."

Sarah glanced around. *Good grief, when had it gotten light?* The sun was topping the mountains.

"Kaycee! What would make you think that?" Sarah asked with an air of innocence.

"I'm not blind. Anyway, Claire's about ten minutes away with Wyatt. Do you want her to keep him here? It's her day to watch him anyway."

One look at Cimarron made Sarah want to tell Kaycee to keep him another night. "No, it's okay if he comes home. Thanks." Sarah disconnected.

"What?" Cimarron said.

"Wyatt's on his way. I need to get going."

"I hate for the night to end." He gave her a long kiss. "We'll talk about the house later."

"Okay. I have to go to Bozeman this afternoon. Do you want to ride along? Café business. Pretty boring stuff, but you're welcome to come."

"Wish I could. I made a couple of appointments with local building-supply owners, to line up materials when I need them."

"Sounds like you were planning on doing this restoration anyway, whether I wanted you to or not," she said, a hint of resentment shadowing the memory of the wonderful night. "Did you think I couldn't get the money?"

"I never said that, Sarah. I just like to look ahead. If I end up not doing any more work, I won't place the orders. Right now, I'm finding a supplier I like. Now scoot before we get caught red-handed."

CHAPTER EIGHTEEN

CIMARRON FINISHED his business and was back at the café before Sarah returned. He stopped by the clinic to see if Wyatt wanted to come home with him, but the twins and a couple of the Rider girls were there, and Cimarron knew he couldn't pry the boy away. No matter, he had plenty to do in the house, so he grabbed a sandwich and a bottle of water and headed up there.

He'd been working about an hour, sanding the repairs he and Sarah had made, when he heard Splinter give a menacing growl behind him. He'd left the dog sleeping outside the apartment. He eased around to see if she'd turned on the hand that fed her. She crouched near the foyer arch, her hackles up, ears focused like radar on something outside the house.

Heavy footsteps grew louder. The dog rose to attack position as Deputy Griff Whitman came through the door.

"Down," Cimarron ordered. Splinter reluctantly dropped to the floor, but her eyes locked on the stranger.

"What the...?" Griff reached for his nightstick.

The dog snarled as he raised the stick.

Cimarron stepped between the animal and the deputy.

"There's no need for that. She's not going to bother you."

"Your dog?"

"My dog."

"She had her shots?"

"Yes. She's wearing tags."

"Good thing or she'd be off to the pound."

Cimarron's dislike of this smart-ass jacked up a few notches. "Is that all you wanted? Because I've got a lot of work to do."

"I don't think Sarah's going to want you to do much more here."

Cimarron tamped down his irritation with great effort. No need to get the local law on his case, since he intended to stay a while, but from the looks of things Deputy Dawg had already targeted him. "What makes you say that?"

"Because when Sarah buys this house back, she's going to hire somebody else to finish it."

Was that what she was trying to tell him this morning? And last night? That she wanted him gone. Boy, if it was, he'd lost his knack for reading women. Besides, he wasn't taking anything verbatim from this jerk. Sarah would have to tell him that herself.

"Why do you think Sarah's going to buy the house back? That's a lot of money to come up with."

"Yeah, I know how you hiked the price up on her. That didn't sit well with a lot of people around here. But that's neither here nor there anymore. I told her night before last that I'd give her the money for it. And the money to fix it up."

Cimarron frowned. Where would a deputy sheriff in this podunk town get that kind of money? Just showed, a book couldn't be judged by the cover. Nonetheless, it put a major crimp in Cimarron's plans. And forced him to rethink what he'd heretofore considered a perfect night, with the promise of more to come.

"You may not know this, but Sarah and I went together for a couple of years. We broke up over some piddling misunderstanding, but all that's behind us and I'm going to do whatever it takes to get her back. Even buy this heap of rubbish because she wants it so much."

Griff slapped the nightstick against his thigh menacingly. Splinter growled deep in chest and Cimarron spoke to her again.

"So, basically what I'm telling you is, you and that kid of yours can pack up and go any time."

His words made Cimarron angry enough, but the thought of Sarah and Deputy Dawg together set his mind to seething and ramped up his blood pressure significantly. He forced himself to answer civilly, since he didn't want to give Griff any reason to lock him up.

"I believe I'll wait until I have Sarah's name on a sales contract and the money has cleared at the bank." He jerked his head toward the door as an invitation for the deputy to leave. "Now I have work to do."

"Start packing." Griff gave the dog another glare, then stalked away.

Cimarron rubbed his chin in aggravation. Something cold and wet touched his other hand. Splinter whined. He squatted and tousled her ears. "It's all right, girl. He's gone. We soon may be, too."

The dog pressed her nose to his cheek, as if she understood. She wagged her tail, but her eyes darted nervously between him and the door.

His mood dampened by Griff's unwanted visit, Cimarron walked to the front porch. Just then Sarah drove up and parked under her carport. Cimarron started down the hill to talk to her, but Griff appeared from the direction of the parking lot, where he'd apparently been waiting for her, and they went inside the door leading to her apartment.

Cimarron recalled Sarah telling him she could be nice to anybody for a month. Well, it had almost worked. Almost. Too bad Deputy Dawg blew it for her, after all her hard work.

Cimarron went to the clinic and fetched Wyatt. After they both cleaned up, they drove to Bozeman for a movie and dinner—guys night, he said when Wyatt asked if Sarah was coming. Cimarron had no intention of sitting around while Sarah carried on with her old beau a few yards away.

And he might just charge her for every damn nail he had driven into that house. On the ride home, he whacked the steering wheel with his hand, waking Wyatt from his snooze.

"Are we home?" Wyatt asked.

"Not yet."

"Are you mad at me, Unca Cimron?"

"No, why do you ask?"

"You sound mad."

"Not with you. Did you like the movie?"

"It was good. I like the big picture. My daddy took me to some movies, but mostly he brought them home for the TV."

"I guess that's a lot easier."

"We don't even have a TV at Sarah's. I didn't even think about it till now."

"Me neither," Cimarron said. "I haven't had a TV in years."

"It's more fun without it. I like coloring and stories better that having to watch TV all the time."

"Me, too."

"You're a good daddy, Unca Cimron."

Cimarron's throat caught and for a minute he couldn't speak. Finally, he managed to say, "I appreciate that, Wyatt." But he knew that opinion was subject to change over the next few days.

. . . .

FROM HER WINDOW, Sarah watched and waited for Cimarron to return. It was almost midnight and she couldn't figure out where he'd gone without saying a word. Claire told her he had picked Wyatt up early. They must have left in the truck while she was getting rid of Griff. Seemed he thought offering her money somehow reopened the door to their old relationship, even though she hadn't accepted his offer. Now she understood exactly how high a return on investment Griff expected. Finally she gave up her vigil and went to bed to get a few hours' sleep. More than ever, she wanted to work out a solution with Cimarron, but she wouldn't have a break at the café until noon.

The next morning, Sarah checked to be sure Cimarron's truck was parked in its usual place near the apartment. She must have slept soundly because she hadn't heard him come home. The apartment was dark, and she went to work hoping to catch him if he came in for breakfast or, if not then, in the afternoon.

The lunch crowd cleared out and cleanup was almost done, when Sarah heard Wyatt outside playing with Splinter. She left Aaron to finish.

She wiped her hands clean and stepped onto the deck. Wyatt wore a long-sleeved buttoned shirt, khaki pants and his old scuffed boots. Sarah tucked a note into the back of her mind: cowboy boots for Christmas or his birthday, whichever came first. He threw a toy for Splinter, who happily retrieved it time after time.

"Hi, Wyatt," Sarah said, joining him on the ground.

"Hey."

"You're all dressed up today. Going somewhere?"

"Unca Cimron has a meeting in Bozeman. I have to go, too, since Claire's not here."

"Oh, well, that sounds like fun, I guess."

Wyatt pulled a face. "Not really. I don't want to go, but Unca Cimron says he don't have a choice."

"I guess you could stay with me if you wanted to."

The little boy brightened instantly. "Could I really? I don't want to go to that meeting."

"Let's ask."

Wyatt ran ahead, catching Cimarron as he came out of the apartment. He was dressed to the nines, as well, in a dark suit, red power tie and light blue shirt. His hair was combed as neatly as those black curls could manage, and his highly polished shoes glistened. Certainly not the carpenter look he usually sported. Sarah gave a wolf whistle.

"Wow, you two look like fashion models. What's the occasion?"

"Meeting," Cimarron said without further elaboration. He handed Wyatt the backpack in which he kept his toys.

Sarah hesitated. Did she detect a little hostility? Maybe more than a little? But why? They'd parted on the very best of terms. Unless he hadn't put the same significance on their night together. Leading the vagabond life that he did, he might have spent nights like that with many women. One-night stands. Easy come, easy go. But he sure hadn't acted that way...

"Is something wrong?" she asked.

He lifted a shoulder; a gesture Sarah had seen before when he didn't want to talk. "What would be wrong?"

"I don't know, you just seem out of sorts."

"Don't worry about it. Come on, Wyatt."

"But, Unca Cimron, Sarah says I can stay with her."

Cimarron gave her an inscrutable look, then took Wyatt's hand. "You'd better come with me."

"Why? He's perfectly welcome to stay."

"Please, Unca Cimron, please? I don't want to sit with a sec'tary while you meet."

"That's crazy, Cimarron. Let him stay here and play. He won't be in the way. I thought we might bake cookies."

Wyatt gave his uncle a beseeching look.

"I guess it would be better all around," Cimarron conceded. "Mind Sarah, understand?"

"I will." Wyatt pulled his hand free and took Sarah's. "I like cooking," he said to Sarah.

"You do? When did you cook?"

"Unca Cimron and I made cheese sandwiches one night. They were good."

She glanced at Cimarron, who smiled at Wyatt but not her. What was wrong with him this morning?

"Save me a cookie," he said.

"I will," Wyatt promised.

Cimarron drove off without another word. Sarah watched his truck go out of sight. Perplexed, she led Wyatt inside.

"What kind of cookies are we going to bake?" he asked.

"What kind do you like?"

"Chocolate chip or oatmeal. Any kind, really." He set his toys aside in a corner.

"How about my famous chocolate chip–oatmeal cookies."

"Oh, boy. Can you do that?"

"Sure can. Wash your hands and then climb up here." She pulled a step stool over to the counter to bring him up to the right height and set out the baking sheets, bowls and ingredients.

She creamed together butter, granulated and brown sugar and vanilla in a large bowl, then beat in the eggs one at a time. She handed a bowl with premeasured flour, baking soda and salt in it to Wyatt, along with a small scoop.

"When I tell you to, I want you to dump a little of the flour into my bowl so I can mix it up. Okay?"

"Okay." He dug out a scoop of flour. Sarah moved the beaters aside.

"Now, just a little."

He dumped a tiny bit.

"A bit more than that."

He tried again.

"Perfect." She beat the flour in, then pushed the beaters to the side. "Again."

They repeated the process until all the flour had been incorporated into a rich, gooey dough.

"Now the nuts."

"Squirrels eat nuts," he commented as he poured.

"That's right. Where did you learn that?"

"Unca Cimron read me a book about animals."

"Do you like books?"

Wyatt nodded vigorously. "I like to color, too. I brought my crayons and coloring book. Do you like to color, Miss Sarah?"

"Well, yes, I used to. We can color while the cookies bake, if you'd like." She'd probably have to get busy prepping for dinner before Cimarron returned, but she still had some time left.

She gave Wyatt a spoon and took one herself, and together they dropped the cookie dough onto the shining baking sheet. His small, smooth hands and the frowning concentration on his face fascinated Sarah as he put each spoonful of dough exactly where he thought it should go. Cimarron's brow knitted like that when he concentrated, too, she'd noticed. And his unruly hair curled over his collar like his nephew's, and he often glanced her way while he worked, just as Wyatt did now.

A tiny Cimarron. Sarah smiled, and then the smile faded as she recalled his odd behavior today. She placed the baking sheets in the preheated oven and wiped her hands clean. She handed Wyatt a damp paper towel so he could do the same.

"Where's your coloring book?"

He pulled a thick book from his backpack, along with a huge carton of crayons, the kind Sarah had loved as a child, with the built-in sharpener and every color imaginable to a child. At least Cimarron had equipped the boy with the best in toys.

The book had connect-the-dots, find the hidden object, shapes, mazes and other game pages, in addition to coloring pages with everything from animals, to people, to cars and landscapes. A lot of thought had gone into choosing that book.

"Do you want to do games or color?" Wyatt asked.

"Which do you want to do?"

"This number game. But will you do it with me? I don't know all my numbers yet. Unca Cimron's teaching me. I can say my ABCs, though," he said proudly.

"That's great." Had this child been taught nothing until a couple months ago? "Did your daddy teach you any numbers or words?"

"No, he was always too tired, and Erica always had a headache and couldn't read."

"Let's play the game."

The game alternately gave the spelling or the numeral and the player had to fill in the mate. Wyatt recognized the numerals, but couldn't read the words for the numbers, so Sarah patiently taught him to read one through ten as they filled in the blanks.

"I missed you guys last night," Sarah said, shamelessly fishing for information.

"We went to a movie and got some hamburgers in Bozeman."

"Oh, was it a good movie?"

"It was great. A cartoon with animals in it."

"Sounds good."

"I told Unca Cimron to ask you to come, but he said you had company."

"Company?" Griff. So that's what had Cimarron's nose out of joint. He'd seen Griff's car. Men!

"I wish he'd called me. I would have gone."

"Maybe we'll go again."

"I hope so."

Next they found a double spread with a coloring scene on each page. Sarah's was a landscape, which she liked, and Wyatt's had three puppies, one standing, one sitting and one curled up in sleep. She watched with interest as Wyatt colored the sleeping puppy brown with markings like Splinter's, then scribbled z's going up from its mouth.

"What's that?" she asked.

"She's sleeping," he said. "That's snoring. Unca Cimron showed me how that meant snoring. He snores, you know. He said all real men snore."

Sarah couldn't stop the laughter that sprang from her lips. "He said that?"

"Yes, ma'am." Wyatt chuckled. "He makes lots of noises when he sleeps sometimes." Wyatt made a snoring sound, then a snort.

Sarah looked forward to learning those night noises peculiar to Cimarron and to know the warmth of his body next to her when she woke in the night, and...and...everything! She just wanted to be with him all the time, in every way.

The buzzer on the stove blared. "Cookies are ready. I'll get them, and you finish your picture."

When the cookies had cooled enough, she took a plate to the table. Wyatt had started on another coloring page. He stopped to take a cookie and eat it, licking his lips afterward in appreciation. He took a sip of milk and went back to coloring, but Sarah could tell something was on his mind. After a few minutes of diligent coloring, with another cookie break, he lowered his head close to the page, and said quietly, "Do you know where Unca Cimron went today?"

"I'm not sure. Do you know?"

"I think he went to get somebody to 'dopt me."

Sarah's lips parted in surprise. For a moment she was dumbstruck. "To do what?"

"'Dopt me. Like I have to go live somewhere else."

Surely she was not hearing this child right.

"Why do you think that?"

"I heard him talking about it on the phone. And he talked to me about some other families who wanted little boys. Where there'd be a mom and a dad all the time."

Sarah struggled to keep her composure and sound calm. "What do you think about that, Wyatt?"

The small shoulders lifted slightly. "I don't know. If they're nice, I guess it'd be okay. And Unca Cimron doesn't love me, so maybe somebody else might."

"Don't say that, Wyatt. Of course he loves you."

"My daddy kinda said that Unca Cimron don't love none of his family except my grandmama that died a long time ago."

"Wyatt, listen to me." She lifted the sad face up toward her. "Your uncle loves you very much. If he is looking into another family for you to live with, it's because he does love you and wants you to have a happy life. He lives by himself and he works all over the place, and you couldn't go with him on all those jobs he does. I think he must want you to have a nice home and two parents and make friends and go to school."

"That's kinda what he said, too." Wyatt pulled away and went back to coloring.

Sarah moved quietly around the kitchen, cleaning the equipment they'd used and clearing things away to have room to prepare dinner when Aaron came in half an hour. Her heart bore down inside her like an iron weight and she took deep breaths to keep from crying. Wyatt did need a good home, but it should be with Cimarron—and her. If he went back to his old lifestyle, the child would be jerked from place to place without putting down roots or making lasting friends. No chance for a real home, or a mother. So in that respect Cimarron was right on target about the adoption.

But it still felt so very, very wrong.

CHAPTER NINETEEN

THE MEETING WENT too well and Cimarron couldn't find any real fault with the Carringtons that he could use as an excuse to call everything off. The prospective parents had adopted other older children, including an international child, so they had already met every requirement necessary. Which meant the adoption could proceed quickly, if the couple liked Wyatt and thought he would fit into their family—and, of course, if he seemed likely to warm up to them.

They pressed Cimarron to bring Wyatt to a fast-food place in Livingston the following week so they could see him, and if the time seemed right, for Wyatt to meet them. Reluctantly, Cimarron agreed to think about it. Right now he would have paid a king's ransom for a crystal ball to see what the future would hold for Wyatt either way. If he could just feel confident that he could do the job right, there would be no question about what his decision would be. But he had to admit that the Carringtons would make excellent parents for Wyatt.

When Cimarron went in through the back door of the café, Wyatt was playing at a table out of the way while Sarah and Aaron worked. He jumped up and ran to Cimarron.

"Did you have fun?" Cimarron asked.

"Yep. And we saved you a cookie!" He pulled a bag from behind his back filled with delicious-smelling cookies. Cimarron took it and hefted it. "Feels like more than one."

Wyatt nodded vigorously. "I saved me one, too, and Sarah put some more in there for us."

"That was nice of her."

From the grim set of Sarah's lips, however, Cimarron gathered the afternoon hadn't gone all that well. So what? His hadn't been a walk in the park, either.

"Thanks for letting him stay, Sarah," he said.

She turned over her task of stirring gravy to Aaron and crossed the room. "Wyatt, don't you want to run outside and see if Splinter's around. Here, I've got a treat for her." She went to the refrigerator to pull out a large ham bone in a storage bag.

"Thanks!" He scampered out the door, bag in hand.

"We need to talk," Sarah said.

"Sure. Did he do something bad?"

"In here." She opened the door to the hallway leading to her apartment. "Aaron, will you keep an eye on Wyatt for a couple of minutes, please?"

She followed Cimarron into the hallway and closed the door. A flight of stairs led up to the apartment Cimarron had never seen, even if Griff had...The seething anger stirred again. Another door led to the deck outside.

"What did he do?" Cimarron asked.

"*He* didn't do anything. It's what you're doing!" Sarah's eyes glinted with rage and her voice trembled.

"What am I doing?"

"Putting that precious child up for adoption."

Cimarron swallowed hard. He hadn't eaten all day, and a thready queasiness twisted his gut into knots. "How do you know about that?"

"Wyatt said that's where you were today. Putting him up for adoption. He overheard your phone conversations." Then Sarah repeated what R.J. had told Wyatt. "He's a very bright little boy. He's trying so hard to be good and fit in, but he thinks you don't love him."

"That's not true. I just want to make sure I do what's best for him."

"Well, as far as Wyatt knows it's the truth. Have you once told him you loved him since you've had him?"

The knot in Cimarron's stomach wrapped around his chest like a constrictor. And frankly, he'd rather have faced a monster python than answer that question. His silence proved enough for Sarah.

"I thought not."

"I'm just not good at that. I...I...My folks...They just never..." He fell silent, the agony of his past rising up to taint his life and his future. Why couldn't he open up to Sarah? Of all people, he wanted most for her to understand. And help him.

"And now you're putting him up for adoption."

"That's not what I was doing today. Not exactly."

"What does that mean? 'Not exactly.'"

Cimarron ran a hand across his mouth, trying to squelch the roil of guilt, defensiveness and anger warring in his gut.

"Look, I started this process weeks ago, when I first got him, because I didn't think I could take care of him. The lawyer pressed me to at least meet the Carringtons, because I probably couldn't find a better family. And he's right."

"You didn't give Wyatt much time, did you? Is that how you deal with all your relationships? Cut and run, as fast as you can?"

"It used to be, yes," he admitted hesitantly. "But—"

"But what? Suddenly, you've changed?"

Cimarron held up his hands in a gesture of frustration. "You don't think somebody can change, Sarah? You may be right. I noticed how quick you went back to your old ways."

"Excuse me?"

"Griff. I saw him at your apartment last night."

"He dropped by. So? One night with you and I can't even talk to an old friend?"

"Old *boy*friend. Who's going to lay out a couple of million dollars to redo your damn house. What does he expect in return for that kind of favor?"

"I cannot believe you are standing there saying this. How dare you?"

Cimarron had heard tales of redheaded furies, and now he believed every word. He expected Sarah to tear into him tooth and claw any second. Although he was so emotionally torn up already that he wasn't sure he'd notice. "I dare, because your boyfriend came by yesterday and told me he was giving you the money and you were getting back together. He basically gave me my walking papers as far as that house goes. Then you were with him last night and..."

"For about fifteen minutes, for heaven's sake." Sarah's voice rose a few notches and she poked him in the chest with her finger to punctuate every sentence. "If you'd hung around long enough, you'd have known that. I intended to turn him down because I thought you and I were starting something good. But I've changed my mind. Because, Cimarron Cole, I don't want anything to do with a man who would turn his back on a sweet, innocent child like Wyatt. You whined because your daddy ran out on you? And now you're doing the same thing? At least you had a mother and a brother. Wyatt doesn't have anybody."

Up to that point Cimarron might have had an argument, but her words cut to his soul and the fight went out of him. He'd never wanted to be compared to his father in any way. Especially not this way. Not by somebody he loved.

He'd convinced himself early on that he was doing what was best for Wyatt. Not deserting him like Jackson Cole had done his family. Not relegating Wyatt to a life of anxiety, poverty and insecurity. He was going to find a stable, solid family—like the Carringtons—to give Wyatt a wonderful life. Not the same thing at all, in his mind. Yet to Sarah it was just as bad.

Cimarron shook his head, fighting down sickening self-revulsion. He barely heard Sarah's continuing rant as he retreated to the outer-hall door.

"No, I'm not going back to Griff. But I might take his money now, just to get you off my property and out of my life. And I might raze that house to the ground because I won't be able to look at it anymore without thinking about what happened to Wyatt."

When Cimarron finally found his tongue, he hardly recognized his own shaky voice. "You're damn right. You don't want anything to do with a man like me. You deserve better." He opened the door behind him. "And so does Wyatt."

She caught him by the arm.

"You know, Cimarron, you have this major martyr complex, and you need to lose it."

"What the hell are you talking about?"

"You say you're not a good enough daddy, so you'll give up Wyatt to a better family. You're not good enough for me, and so you'll give me up to somebody better. Well, damn it, I don't think that's what you really want to do. I think you love Wyatt better than anything and I think you care about me, and I don't believe for a minute you want to leave either of us behind."

He jerked away from her. "It's not a matter of what I want," he said. "Never has been."

This time he left before she could stop him.

• • • •

THROUGH THE LONG HOURS until the café closed that night, Sarah worked by rote, her mind churning. More than once, Aaron asked if something was wrong, and each time she said no. But something *was* wrong. Her world had suddenly shifted beneath her like an earthquake, throwing her off balance. A chasm had opened, leaving her on one side and Cimarron and Wyatt on the other. She wanted to reach out and pull them back to her, but she didn't know how.

She hadn't meant to yell at him like she did, but when he made those totally off-base remarks about her and Griff she lost her temper. She cringed every time she remembered his stricken expression and the horror in his eyes when she compared him to his father. She never should have done that, and now she couldn't take back the hurtful words. In his mind he was trying to do the right thing by the child but in her heart she knew he was making the wrong decision. For all of them.

When at last she locked the doors to the building, she went to her bedroom and sat by the window, staring down at the dark apartment, wondering if Cimarron and Wyatt were asleep or if solace was as elusive for Cimarron as it was proving for her.

Every time she thought about Wyatt, she wanted to cry. He loved his uncle and she loved them both, but she was angry that Cimarron had jumped to conclusions about her and Griff without even giving her the benefit of the doubt. And when he left he seemed more determined than ever to go through with his plans.

So be it. He'd made his bed, he'd have to lie in it—alone, as far as she was concerned. She glanced at the clock. Eleven. Late, but probably not too late. Picking up the phone, she dialed.

When the voice came on the other end, she said, "Just the man I wanted to talk to. I want to take you up on your offer to help me buy back my house, if it still stands."

"Of course it does. Whatever I can do to help you out."

"Can we get together tomorrow and talk? I hate to ask you to come here, but I have to work all day."

"No problem. What time?"

"Around two would be good. Thanks."

She held the receiver in her hands long after the call ended. She wasn't sure she was doing the right thing, either, but at least she could begin to put this upheaval behind her.

• • • •

THE NEXT MORNING Cimarron and Wyatt sat down to breakfast in the tiny apartment that had become a temporary haven for both of them. Cimarron jacked up his courage as the child ate his cereal.

"Wyatt, Miss Sarah told me that you know where I went yesterday."

Wyatt looked up with wide eyes almost black with dread. "Yes, sir. I heard you talk about it on the phone."

"Do you understand why I want a good home for you?"

The child pursed his lips and looked away from Cimarron.

"You can be honest. We're buddies, you know that."

Wyatt heaved a big sigh. "You don't love me and don't want me."

"That's not true, Wyatt." Cimarron said, struggling to keep his composure. "Sometimes we have to make hard decisions no matter how we feel about somebody."

"But why do you want to 'dopt me?" Wyatt still held his dripping spoon over the cereal bowl but wasn't eating now.

Cimarron sat back wearily, his own breakfast untouched. He pushed both hands through his hair then leaned forward with his forearms crossed on the table. "Wyatt, I...I'm by myself and don't have anybody to help me out."

A hopeful look crossed Wyatt's round face. "I could help you, Unca Cimron, and be here with you."

Cimarron slumped. "No, I mean I don't have anybody to look after you. I travel a lot with my work and you couldn't go with me then, because I wouldn't have any way to take care of you. Or you'd have to move around with me and change schools every year, and that's not a good thing."

"I don't go to school."

"Not yet, but you will soon. If you were in a family with a mother and a father, they would put you in a good school and you'd make a lot of friends."

"I have friends. I like Zach and Tyler and I don't want any other friends."

"I know. But you'll like the new friends in time."

Wyatt crossed his arms and pouted. "No, I won't!"

"You'll be surprised. The bottom line is that I can't give you the right kind of home. I can't raise you like I want you to be raised."

Cimarron swallowed hard, then admitted, "I just wouldn't be a good daddy for you, buddy."

Wyatt's curly head ducked low over his cereal. Cimarron almost took him in his arms and recanted everything he'd just said. But he forced himself to be strong and let the child go on to a better life, especially now that Sarah was out of the picture. He pushed away from the table and took his own untouched breakfast plate outside, giving the food to Splinter.

All work ceased on the house. After that day, Cimarron kept a wide berth of the café and anyplace else he might run into Sarah. He was surprised she hadn't kicked them out of the apartment yet, but that probably was due to her fondness for Wyatt.

Wyatt grew more withdrawn as the days passed. Cimarron needed to make a decision, good or bad, and get it done, so that Wyatt could begin to heal—again. He arranged a meeting with the Carringtons on an afternoon when Claire was available. Cimarron invited her and the twins to go along, hoping Wyatt would be more at ease with his friends.

He didn't consider asking Sarah. In fact, he chose a day when he knew she'd have to work. He didn't want to be in her presence, to feel her disappointment in him. Once the adoption was final, he'd be gone, and Sarah would be just another woman in his past. *In your dreams,* he thought—*literally.* She would never be like the others, no matter how he tried to fool himself.

With the youngsters belted into the backseat of Cimarron's truck, Claire did most of the talking on the ride to Livingston. Her youthful eagerness concerning her plans for a therapeutic-riding school struck Cimarron and made him wonder if he'd ever been that unconditionally excited about anything. Maybe not as a youth, but he knew he had been. Just recently. Over Sarah and the possibility of a future with her and Wyatt. That feeling had given way to a constant heaviness of mind and spirit. Knowing that soon he would be alone in the world once more added to the burden.

"How close are you to opening?" Cimarron asked, trying to shake off his gloom. He'd watched Claire give lessons and knew she would be a perfect teacher for challenged children.

"Oh, a year maybe. I have to save money, and I can't work full-time until I finish school this semester. And I need to find good horses to train. Kaycee will give me the space free, thank goodness."

"How much are the horses?"

"Depends. I'm hoping to get five good ones for under fifteen thousand. And my helpers will be volunteers. I'm so anxious to get started, but I'm forcing myself to be patient."

"That's smart. No need to rush, with school left to finish." Cimarron hesitated, then said, "I appreciate you coming with me today. You've been a godsend to Wyatt and me. Let me help you out with a donation to your school. Maybe enough to buy a couple of those horses you need."

"Are you sure? That's a lot of money."

"I give to worthy causes every year. Tax breaks, you know. We'll work on the details later."

"Oh, that's wonderful! I can't thank you enough," Claire said, the radiance in her face the only thanks Cimarron really needed.

They pulled into the parking lot and the boys jumped down as soon as they were released from their seat belts and ran inside.

Cimarron had explained to Claire about the meeting and the Carringtons when he asked her to come.

"I hope it works out and he can settle down." She said it without criticism, but Cimarron felt the knife of guilt cut ever deeper with every step he took toward this adoption. He'd always trusted his instinct, but this time, too much was at stake. If he made the wrong decision...

Cimarron and Claire entered behind the boys and Cimarron glanced around until he saw the couple, Don and Amy Carrington, sitting in a corner booth. Both were dressed casually. Don wore jeans, running shoes and a yellow knit shirt, and Amy's stylish sweater and khakis complemented her trim figure. Cimarron gave them a slight nod and they returned the gesture. They had arranged a signal beforehand to let him know if they wanted to meet Wyatt face-to-face, and Cimarron would acknowledge it if he felt the child was ready. He had not told Wyatt the Carringtons would be here, but he had a feeling the boy was suspicious about this meeting.

After a burger, fries and a toy, the youngsters were ready to hit the playground. Cimarron and Claire followed them out and a minute or so later the Carringtons took a seat nearby.

Claire sipped a Coke, but Cimarron had no appetite. He hadn't eaten more than a bite at a time over the past week. Until he'd arrived in Little Lobo his stomach hadn't acted up so much since his mother died. Anyway, the nerves were back now with a vengeance and the wrenching pain probably wouldn't go away until he put his taillights to this place.

He glanced toward the Carringtons, and Don gave him the signal. Cimarron watched Wyatt play for a couple more minutes, then told the boys to take a break. He sent Claire and the twins to bring back ice cream and Claire knew she was to take her time. The Carringtons moved to the table next to theirs.

"I want you to meet some people, Wyatt."

Wyatt paled and moved quickly to stand on the far side of Cimarron. He wrapped an arm around his uncle's knee as Cimarron introduced them. He'd had a couple of long phone conversations with the Carringtons in recent days and had seen photos of their home on the outskirts of Bozeman, a rambling two-story home on a generous lot. The house appeared prosperous but not stuffy. The Carringtons themselves were pleasant, well spoken and showed a true interest in the welfare of their children, which might soon include Wyatt.

"Hi, Wyatt," Amy said. "Are you having a good time?"

"Yes, ma'am."

"Are those twins your friends?"

"Yes, ma'am."

Cimarron was on pins and needles, alternately wanting Wyatt to talk and make a good impression, and then finding that he hoped he didn't. But why? That would only mean more searching, more time lost getting Wyatt settled.

"We have five children," Amy said. "Two are about your age. One is from China. Do you know where that is?"

Wyatt shook his head. "Do you live in China?"

Don chuckled. "No, Wyatt, we live in Bozeman, a few miles from here."

"I've been to Bozeman." Wyatt shifted from foot to foot and looked toward the door for his playmates.

"Do you like to ride horses?" Don asked.

Wyatt nodded. "My daddy was a rodeo rider."

"So I heard. I don't do rodeo, but we have some nice horses and ponies to ride. And a swimming pool. Do you like to swim?"

"Don't know how."

"Well, it's fun when you learn. Think you'd like to learn?"

Wyatt shrugged. "Guess so. Do you have dogs?"

"No, no dogs. One of our children is allergic to dogs, so we can't have any."

"I like dogs," Wyatt said, his expression troubled now. "I have a dog at Unca Cimron's."

"I wish we could have a dog," Don said.

Wyatt brightened when Claire returned with the twins and ice-cream cones for everyone.

"Can I go play with Zach and Tyler now?" Wyatt asked, turning pleading eyes up to Cimarron.

"Sure, run along."

"He's very polite," Amy commented when Wyatt was out of earshot.

"Yes, he's a good boy," Cimarron said. "And smart. He understands what's going on."

Don grew serious. "Are you having second thoughts? Because it looks like the two of you have a good relationship."

"I think we do, but I can't provide all he needs."

"Love?" Amy said. "That's really the most important part of being a family."

"In this case, I'm not sure love is enough. I want him to have a good life and a stable home."

Amy smiled. "We can certainly give him that."

The Carringtons left soon afterward. Cimarron allowed the boys to play a while longer before heading home.

The twins cut up all the way, laughing and bickering. But Wyatt never said a word, even when they teased him. Cimarron didn't have anything to say, either, and Claire stared out her window the entire time.

That night the lawyer called. The Carringtons had fallen in love with Wyatt and wanted to start the adoption process as soon as possible. They asked to have Wyatt spend a couple of nights at their house to ease the adjustment.

Holding the receiver to his ear, Cimarron gazed at the sleeping child. A young R.J., who resembled Cimarron enough to be his own son. What was best for this little boy? If he was waiting for divine guidance, it hadn't come so far.

"Sure, that'll be fine," he said, trying to keep the bitterness out of his voice.

He hung up and went outside into the chilly darkness. He couldn't wander with Wyatt sleeping, so he left the door open a crack and sat at the small table on his end of the deck where he could see inside.

The soft night sounds couldn't soothe him as they usually did. He doubted he'd ever have peace of mind again. Or ever be truly free. The ghosts of Wyatt and Sarah would haunt him the rest of his life, along with all the things he'd never get to do with them.

Make love to Sarah, watch her grow with his baby inside her, hold his own child in his arms. And Wyatt...not be around to teach him to fish or ride a bike. To build something beautiful. To play baseball and shoot hoops. Take him to the movies, show him the world. See him turn into a strong, good man. Teach him to drive and buy him his first old truck. Share the exhilaration of his first romantic crush. To stand as best man at his wedding. To go with Sarah to see their first grandchild. To...to...

Cimarron leaned over with his elbows on his knees and put his head in his hands. *Why the hell was he thinking about all that now? And what could he change? Not a damn thing!*

He wanted to talk to somebody, to voice all the pain and guilt. He wanted Sarah more than anything. But the lights in her apartment were out and she would probably tell him to get lost anyway.

These were the times when a man needed family. But if he had a family, he wouldn't be in this predicament. He remembered as a child hearing his mother pray and he thought then how futile it was. Her prayers had never seemed to be answered, yet she never lost faith. She told her skeptical son that the Lord always listened and answered in His own time.

Cimarron raised his head to ponder the black sky, pinpointed by brilliant stars, searching for something he couldn't see and wasn't sure existed.

"Well, God," he said. "I hope You're listening, because I don't have anybody else left, and I don't know what to do."

CHAPTER TWENTY

ALTHOUGH SARAH usually looked forward to the first hint of morning light through her windows, today she was just grateful for an excuse to end a miserable night. She wasn't sure how she'd get through the day with no sleep, but she'd spent the night at her darkened window, watching Cimarron sitting on the deck outside the apartment. She wanted to go down and talk to him, but what was left to say?

Sometime today, her lawyer would call Cimarron to notify him that she had the money for the house and to set up a time for them to sign the contract. Hard to believe that they'd come full circle in the space of a few weeks. From enemies to lovers and back to enemies. She'd have her house but she didn't have the money to restore it, just as he'd predicted.

It would remain as it had been for years, a useless old house on the hill, which would eventually rot to the ground. Tears stung at the thought of all she'd lost and couldn't regain. And sweet little Wyatt. She would never be able to look at that house again without seeing him playing on the porch with Splinter lying beside him, watching over him.

Why didn't you just stay out of my life, Cimarron!

• • • •

CIMARRON HAD WASHED all Wyatt's clothes and had them neatly folded on the bed. The Carringtons would take Wyatt to visit in a couple of days and Cimarron had a meeting with Sarah's lawyer scheduled for tomorrow, so he was packing Wyatt's things now while he had time. When the adoption became final, he'd move from the apartment to the motel until the business with the house was completed. Then he would hit the road to somewhere else. Anywhere else.

He'd thought the days after his mother died were bad, but losing Wyatt and Sarah was infinitely worse. Every muscle in his body ached with tension and he couldn't put two thoughts together. He'd had a long talk with God last night, but God hadn't provided any answers. Figured. What had he expected? A voice booming in the darkness: *Keep Wyatt. Beg Sarah back.*

Right. No heavenly voices for him.

Where was Wyatt, anyway? He'd told the boy to gather his toys and books, but they were still scattered across the floor. He had a flash of Wyatt at the top of the ladder, of him teetering off the rock into the steam. Cimarron hadn't noticed him slipping away. No telling what he might be into now. Cimarron rushed to the doorway, only to be stopped short by Wyatt's soft voice. The child sat on the ground, his arm looped around Splinter's neck.

"I gotta go away soon, Splinner," he said.

The dog thumped her tail slowly and Wyatt rubbed her head. "I asked Mr. Carrington if I could bring you, but he said no. Somebody was 'lergic to dogs, whatever that is."

Splinter licked his face.

"I don't want to leave you and Unca Cimron, but he don't want me much, and since my daddy died I'm nobody's little boy anymore."

He hugged the dog tightly and she whined as if she understood.

"I told Unca Cimron I like 'em okay, the Carringtons, but I love you and Unca Cimron better and I don't want to go. How come Unca Cimron don't love me, Splinner? How come?"

Cimarron fought back the sting behind his eyes and gritted his teeth so hard his jaw hurt.

Wyatt buried his face in the dog's rough fur.

"I'm scared, Splinner," he sobbed. "I'm so scared."

If he knew anything, Cimarron knew what it felt like to be a scared kid. And he knew at once that he had to take the fear away from this little boy.

"Wyatt," he called softly.

Wyatt hastily scrubbed the tears away with his shirtsleeve. "I'm coming to get my stuff together."

"No, you don't have to. You're not going anywhere."

Wyatt's small hands were balled into fists and he was trying desperately not to cry. Cimarron knew that feeling, too. Hot tears stung his own eyes and he dug his fingernails painfully into his palms.

"But you said...You said..."

"I know what I said. But I was wrong. You don't need another family. We're a family, you and me. Maybe not the best in the world, and we're going to have some rough spots. But I...I really want you to stay with me. If you want to." Cimarron blinked hard and stooped to the child's level. "I love you, Wyatt, I swear I do. And I'll be the best daddy I can be."

Wyatt flew into Cimarron's outstretched arms, sobbing. "I want to stay. I want to stay! I'll be good."

Cimarron held him at arm's length. "You're always good, son. It's never been you..."

Wyatt grabbed him around the neck and hugged him tight, refusing to let go as Cimarron stood.

"Let's go tell Sarah. You want to?"

Wyatt nodded vigorously against Cimarron's neck.

Cimarron held no hope of reconciling with Sarah now that Griff was back in the picture with money for the house dangling before her like a carrot. But he wanted to redeem himself in her eyes if he could.

Sarah was busy writing the specials of the day on the big board behind the counter. She turned when Wyatt called to her.

"You tell her," Cimarron said to Wyatt.

"I get to stay with Unca Cimron!"

"Really?" She directed the question to Cimarron.

He nodded. "Really. I didn't like being a martyr."

"And I didn't like you being one," she said with a beautiful smile that made Cimarron pine for what he couldn't have.

Maybe this was a bad idea. Probably he should have just left without seeing her again, because now he didn't want to go.

"That's so wonderful, Wyatt! That's the way it should be."

"My unca Cimron loves me. He told me so."

Sarah's eyes brimmed and she grabbed a napkin from the holder on the counter. "I know he does. He'll be a good daddy."

"I...um...I'm glad you got the money for the house," Cimarron said, although he wasn't happy about it. "I'm glad we got some work done on it. Gives you a head start."

"Well, I don't know about that. I don't really have the money to do much with it now. Like you warned me. But under the circumstances...I just didn't want it going to strangers."

"I wouldn't have done that to you, Sarah. I promise. Even though things didn't work out between us like I hoped they would, I wouldn't have sold it out from under you again."

"I appreciate that."

Cimarron nodded. "I hope you can come up with a solution. Griff sounded like he was going to sink enough into the deal for you to fix it up."

"I didn't get the money from Griff."

Cimarron frowned and set Wyatt on the floor. "But I thought. Griff made it pretty clear that—"

"No doubt. I suppose he thought he could run you off. Besides, I know what Griff wanted in return and that was over a long time ago."

"Then how did you get the money?"

"Jon went to bat for me with his banker. He and Kaycee cosigned a loan that I'll pay back somehow. It may take me forever, especially if I never open the bed-and-breakfast."

"Well, it happens I know a pretty good handyman who's out of work right at the moment," Cimarron said, holding her gaze.

Sarah smiled. "Do you, now?"

"Yep."

"Does he work cheap?"

"Not really, but he's willing to make a deal. Maybe good enough you won't need that loan after all." Cimarron stepped around the counter.

"Oh," Sarah said, coming to stand so close they touched. "What kind of a deal?"

"Oh, say, maybe payment in the form of lessons in fathering."

"I could probably help with that." She wrapped her arms around his neck.

"And he has a little boy who needs a good home—and a mother."

She caught her bottom lip in her teeth and traced a finger along Cimarron's jawline, her blue eyes sparkling with the passion he wanted all for himself.

"I'm very family oriented."

He leaned down and nibbled that bottom lip that he loved, then kissed her.

"Can you forgive a reformed martyr enough to marry him?"

She nodded, her loving expression mirroring his feelings.

"You'd better be sure."

He kissed her again. Three times. Four.

Recovering from his flurry of kisses, Sarah drew a deep breath, reached up and brushed the dark curls off his forehead.

"I've never been more sure of anything in my life."

ACKNOWLEDGMENTS

I'D LIKE TO ACKNOWLEDGE several people for their patience and expertise in answering my questions. They graciously gave of their time and knowledge and any misinterpretations or errors belong to me, not them.

Thanks to Bora Sunseri for answering my questions about adoption; Billy Cocreham and the late Otto Buehler for their expertise on construction and restoration; Frank Dedman III for all his help on managing a restaurant; Jim Mayer, Bud Bailey and Mark Pencil for information on and demonstrations of fly-fishing; and Sandra Cahill, 63 Ranch, for answering questions on fly-fishing specific to Montana.

About Elaine

FROM AN EARLY AGE, Elaine wanted to write stories.

Her first short story was published in her small town newspaper when she was in third grade.

Her first novel, *Roses for Chloe*, a Berkley-Jove Haunting Hearts release in 1998 was an RWA RITA Contest finalist. Her next three books were Harlequin Superromance® novels, one of which, *Make Believe Mom*, also went on to become a RITA finalist. Later, Elaine took a leap of faith into indie publishing with her romantic thriller *The Caverns*, the first book in the Tennessee Mountain Home series.

After moving back home to Alabama, Elaine enjoys reconnecting with family and high school friends and visiting her son, daughter-in-law and grands in New York. She lives with her rescue dog Mariah who loves nothing more than chasing squirrels and snakes through the woods.

Elaine's Books

Little Lobo Series – *Heartwarming stories set in the mountains of Montana*
Make-Believe Mom – Book 1
Accidental Dad – Book 2
Along For the Ride – Book 3

Roses For Chloe – *A Louisiana Ghost Story*

The Caverns – *A Romantic Thriller set in the Smoky Mountains of Tennessee*